RETURN TO
THE WINTER PALACE

John Rae has also written:

THE GOLDEN CRUCIFIX

THE TREASURE OF WESTMINSTER ABBEY

CHRISTMAS IS COMING

JOHN RAE

Return to the Winter Palace

ILLUSTRATED BY
SUSAN EDWARDS

HODDER AND STOUGHTON
LONDON SYDNEY AUCKLAND TORONTO

British Library Cataloguing in Publication Data
Rae, John, b.1931
Return to the Winter Palace.
I. Title
823'.9'1J PZ7.R123

ISBN 0-340-21778-2

 First printed 1978. ISBN 0 340 21778 2. Printed in Great Britain for Hodder & Stoughton Children's Books, a division of Hodder & Stoughton Ltd, Mill Road, Dunton Green, Sevenoaks, Kent TN13 2YJ (Editorial Office: 47 Bedford Square, London WC1B 3DP), by T. J. Press (Padstow) Ltd. Phototypeset in V.I.P. Bembo by Western Printing Services Ltd, Bristol.

For
Shamus and Jonathan

One

So this was Russia. Emily sat forward the moment the Ilyushin airliner dropped below the bank of cloud through which it had been flying for twenty minutes or so; and was astonished to see that the world outside the oval window was in darkness. Above the clouds it had been afternoon still, with a clear sky and the sun shining behind the tail of the aircraft. But here it was like a city underground, with a million lights pricking the blackness.

As the aircraft continued its descent, rocking and bumping as though caught by sudden gusts of wind, the lights below acquired a colour and then an identity. The clusters of yellow lights were groups of tall apartment blocks, the lines of pale blue lights were the main roads leading to and from the heart of the city and the single red lights marked the tops of the highest buildings. Emily wondered whether the Russian people below could hear the aircraft sweeping overhead.

She turned to Alyce.

'Fasten your seat belt,' Alyce told her before Emily had a chance to say anything. Alyce was sitting bolt upright gripping the arms of the seat with both hands.

At Gatwick Airport, when Emily had said, 'The bit I like – well, not best, but the bit I like is the aeroplane journey,' Alyce had frowned as though she had known that a journey in a Russian aeroplane was not likely to be a pleasure.

Emily turned back to the window. She made it a rule

never to do straight away what Alyce told her however sensible the instructions might be. Older sisters – of whom Emily had three – had to be kept in their place. Besides there was plenty of time to fasten her seat belt before the aircraft landed. To fasten it now, at the official moment and so far away from touch-down – for no aerodrome was in sight – was contrary to Emily's instincts. It was a kind of cheating, like putting your brakes on the moment your bicycle started down a steep hill. Better to take risks, to leave the brakes as long as you dared, to put your hand in the tiger's cage as she had done as a young girl, receiving a resounding smack from her father even though the tiger had been fast asleep.

The aircraft had left the city now and was flying low over snow-covered open ground. If the pilot was approaching the airport he was certainly going a long way round. But then the snow ended abruptly and the black tarmac of the runway began. Emily fastened her seat belt, pressed the button to bring her seat into the upright position, and looked round at the rest of the family. They did not look at all comfortable. Alyce was staring straight ahead. Beyond her, Penelope was very pale and would certainly be sick if the aircraft did not land soon. On the other side of the gangway, Mummy was sitting with the twins. Shamus was as pale as Penelope, while Jonathan had that distracted air of someone who is trying to think of anything rather than his own stomach.

Emily twisted her head. Surely her eldest sister had not surrendered to the battering of the long descent.

'All right Shiv?' she asked.

Siobhan's voice responded hollowly from the seat behind.

'Yes thanks, darling. You OK?'

'I feel fine,' said Emily. 'Just as well Daddy's not here though; he's always ill.'

'Don't talk about it, Emily,' snapped Alyce.

The wheels hit the tarmac so hard Emily thought the aircraft might fall apart but it rebounded into the air again, flew for a few seconds and then dropped a second time on to the runway. In the passenger cabin, music was played over the loud speakers. The passengers shook their heads and pressed their ears.

'They have good drivers, don't they,' said Shamus loudly.

Penelope folded the reinforced brown paper bag and replaced it in the pocket of the seat in front.

'What does that say?' she asked, still pale and tight-lipped.

Emily counted the Russian letters on the airport building.

'Leningrad,' she replied confidently.

Alyce said: 'You're just guessing, Emily.'

'What's wrong with guessing?' Emily enquired.

The Ilyushin taxied to the parking area, turned in a wide arc and stopped. The passengers stood to put on the expensive winter clothes they had bought in England: heavy pullovers, scarves of different lengths and textures and fur hats with ear flaps that could be worn up or down.

Emily was in no hurry. With the calm detachment of an experienced traveller who knows there will be a long delay before the aeroplane doors are opened, she sat back and watched others struggling in the confined space. When Alyce told her to get a move on, she raised her eyebrows a fraction as though she had heard an unfamiliar sound but did not think it worth investigating. Her mother's instructions could not be treated so lightly however.

'Come on Emily, remember what I said!'

Emily did remember. Their mother – as always – had a plan. She had been to Leningrad before and she knew that those passengers who arrived at the hotel in the first coach were given the rooms with odd numbers which looked out over the River Neva towards the Winter Palace. The even numbered rooms faced the apartment blocks and radio-electronic factories of Leningrad's northern suburbs. The problem – as her mother had explained before they had left home – was to secure seats for the family on the first Intourist coach that left the airport.

Emily pressed her fur hat on to her light brown hair and stooped to study her reflection in the window. She decided that unlike the other passengers she did not look like a tourist; there was something Russian about her fair, freckled face and blue eyes; something Russian and something mysterious. She turned to survey the mere tourists and was surprised to see that her mother was not ready to leave. The aircraft doors opened and the passengers started to press forward but her mother did not budge. She was standing at her seat talking to an upright, elderly lady whose fine, aristocratic features appeared quite unmoved by all the push and bustle. Mummy had a habit – much disapproved of by her children – of talking about the family to strangers.

'Are you coming, Mummy?' Emily asked pointedly as she eased herself into the line of passengers.

'You go ahead, dear, I'll catch you up.'

So much for our plan, Emily thought.

Siobhan and Penelope were way ahead with the twins and soon disappeared through the rear door. Alyce waited for Emily.

'I thought we had a plan,' she said as Emily came up.

'We still do,' said Emily and stepped out into the freezing air.

She had expected the Russian January to be cold but her imagination, even at its most extreme, had not prepared her for this. She set her jaw firmly and with her free hand pressed her fur hat down over her ears. She would not run or call out with surprise like the passengers ahead of her. She descended the steep steps slowly like a monarch coming ashore and walked across the tarmac to the airport building. On either side of the entrance was a soldier in a blue-grey greatcoat and fur hat of matching colour. The soldiers carried automatic rifles and looked straight ahead.

After the bitter cold, the airport building felt almost

oppressively warm. The children gathered in the reception hall while the other passengers passed on to have their passports checked by young soldiers who stood in white cubicles.

'This is hopeless,' said Alyce impatiently. But their mother, when at last she arrived, appeared quite unconcerned at the delay she had caused. She was still talking to the tall, aristocratic lady as though there was no possible reason to hurry.

'Why are you waiting?' she asked the children.

'The twins are on *your* passport,' Siobhan replied with deliberation.

'We shall never get on the first bus at this rate,' said Emily.

'Yes we will,' her mother assured her, 'the luggage is not off the 'plane yet. We shall catch up the other people in the Customs Hall. There's no hurry. And I want you to meet Mrs Hannay. She was born in Leningrad. Isn't that interesting? And she has promised to show us some of the places the Intourist people probably never go to.'

'It is a long time since I was here,' said Mrs Hannay cautiously.

She seemed as embarrassed as the children at their mother's habit of picking up strangers and turning them to the family's advantage.

'Now this is Siobhan . . .' the older children sighed, recognising the opening phrase of their mother's lengthy introduction, 'she's nearly eighteen and she's taking her "A" levels in the summer. Penelope – do hold yourself up straight dear – is fifteen. Alyce is nearly fourteen and Emily, with the dimple, is twelve. Shamus and Jonathan are twins. They look identical, don't they, but they're not. They will be nine in the summer.'

'What a lovely family,' was Mrs Hannay's comment, at which the children groaned audibly, experience having taught them that this was the response their mother's introduction always received. There were times when they wished they could be an awful family, looking like urchins and fighting like cats. The reputation for being a lovely family was a heavy cross to bear.

Emily stared at Mrs Hannay with some resentment. The woman's eyes, she noticed, were a very odd colour that you could not stop looking at because it seemed to be on the point of fading out altogether. It reminded her of the very pale, distant blue of the afternoon sky above the clouds.

Emily went ahead and joined the shortest queue. The instinct to be first was strong even if there was no hurry. But the young soldier, with bare close-cropped head, was taking his time. With each passenger he followed the same slow ritual. He looked at the passport photograph, then at the passenger's face, then – or so it appeared to Emily – down at his boots or at something out of sight, before raising his eyes to search the passenger's face once again. It was all done with a positive lack of urgency.

'Anyone would think they didn't want any tourists,' said the man in front of Emily.

When at length her turn came, Emily could not resist standing on tiptoe and leaning over the narrow shelf on which she had placed her passport to see what it was the soldier had to look down at each time. She saw at once. There was a lower shelf covered with photographs of people, full face, head and shoulders, arranged in tidy rows.

The soldier did not seem to object to her inquisitiveness. The photographs were upside down to Emily but she had an impression of young men with dark features and even darker eyes. Perhaps it was this that made one photograph stand out from the rest. It was the photograph of a woman and even upside down it was a good enough likeness to arrest Emily's casual glance. She turned to look at the woman to whom the family had just been introduced. Then back at the photograph. There was no doubt that the face in the photograph was that of Mrs Hannay.

Two

The photographs were of people wanted by the Russian police. Emily was sure of that. But there was no way of warning Mrs Hannay without alerting the soldier and that was a risk even Emily did not fancy taking. The penalty for helping an enemy of the Soviet Government would be altogether in a different league from the Headmistress's final warning or her parents' passing wrath.

Alyce had already placed her passport on the shelf in front of the young soldier. Emily moved on saying nothing. But while saying nothing satisfied her instinct for survival, it also opened the door to a possible adventure. If Mrs Hannay was refused entry to Russia, that was that, but if by mistake or by design she was allowed to enter, then only Emily would know the secret.

The first pieces of luggage appeared on the conveyor belt and the passengers who had been waiting strolled forward with an air of superior resignation as though they thought it undignified to jostle one another in front of foreigners. Emily moved fast, found her case and lugged it off the conveyor belt on to the floor. It was heavy but not impossible to carry. Alyce was through and Mrs Hannay was next but one to show her passport to the soldier.

'Go on Emily, don't wait,' Alyce called as she waited for her own case to emerge.

'Bossyboots,' murmured Emily but she picked up her case nevertheless.

The customs was a long low table on one side of the hall. The only official on duty was a middle-aged woman whose broad face and heavy build made her appear to Emily a more formidable obstacle than the soldier, for all his uniform and gold stars. She lifted her case on to the table. The customs official indicated that it should be opened. To say that it had been packed would be an exaggeration. Emily had thrown in clothes, hairbrush, sponge-bag, mascots, paperbacks and odds and ends in such a way that when the case was opened the contents were a shambles. The customs official closed the lid herself.

'What is the purpose of your visit?' she asked in a thick, deeply accented voice.

'The what? The purpose? I don't know,' Emily replied and then with a slight narrowing of her deep blue eyes she quoted her mother, 'We're going to see the treasures of Leningrad while it's still possible.'

'How long will you be staying?' the woman asked, obviously quite unimpressed by Emily's performance.

'A week. Everyone's staying a week.'

Emily looked over her shoulder. Mrs Hannay was at this minute standing in front of the young soldier who had her passport in his hand.

'How much English currency do you have?'

Emily watched. Mrs Hannay was erect, holding her chin up. She did not appear at all apprehensive. The soldier was turning the pages of the passport as though looking for irregularities.

'How much English currency . . .'

'Twenty pence,' Emily replied, feeling that, in some way that was not at all clear, she was helping Mrs Hannay by lying to the customs official.

The woman pushed a sheet of white paper over the table.

'You must complete a Currency Declaration Form,' she said, at the same time waving Emily on with a slow gesture of the hand.

Emily did not go far. Mrs Hannay was still facing the soldier but nothing in his expression gave the slightest hint that he had spotted she was the woman in the photograph. He returned her passport without comment. Mrs Hannay picked it up, placed it in her black bag and passed through to collect her luggage.

But Emily watched the soldier still. Mrs Hannay had been the last in his queue but for a while he remained in his white cubicle, looking now and again at the glass doors beyond which the steps to the aeroplane were visible in the snow-blown darkness.

Alyce arrived and Penelope too.

'What are you staring at, Emily?' Alyce demanded.

'Nothing,' Emily replied, but did not take her eyes off the soldier for a second. Other passengers gathered round and she was forced to move to the edge of the group. At last the soldier moved. He opened the side of his cubicle, looked about him and took a packet of cigarettes from the breast pocket of his uniform. One of his colleagues joined him. They stood smoking and chatting in a manner that suggested all was normal. If they knew that a wanted person had entered the country, they were certainly in no hurry to report the fact to their superiors. But that, Emily realised, could be part of the bluff to lull Mrs Hannay into thinking she was safe.

'Hallo,' said a voice near at hand. 'I am Ilsa, your Intourist guide while you are in Leningrad.'

Ilsa was small and pretty with golden hair. She wore a smart, navy-blue suit that was not quite a uniform, with an Intourist badge in the lapel. Her only concessions to the bitter cold outside were furlined boots and a fluffy dome that perched decoratively on the back of her head. She smiled at Emily and Emily smiled back revealing a single dimple in her left cheek.

'So you will come with me now to the first coach,' Ilsa announced, addressing the twenty or so passengers who had cleared customs.

Alyce clicked her tongue.

'We'll have to wait for Mummy,' she said in a despairing tone.

Emily did not give up so easily. They could get on the first coach and save places for Mummy and the others.

'That's all right, isn't it?' she asked Ilsa.

Ilsa replied that there was no problem as each coach could take thirty passengers.

Emily glanced once more at the soldier who had checked their passports before following Ilsa across the main hall of the airport building. The soldier had not moved. Either he had not spotted Mrs Hannay or he had been very well trained in the techniques of deception.

The floor and walls of the main hall were lined with white marble. In a prominent position, opposite the entrance and standing out against the pale background, was a bronze statue of Lenin in a pose that was to become familiar to the children: best foot forward, one hand holding the lapel of his jacket while the other reached out, fist clenched, to drive home some point to the invisible crowd.

The glass doors opened automatically as the first passengers approached. It was half past four in the afternoon, dark as night and several degrees below freezing. Penelope, Alyce and Emily took the front seats on the coach and saved others by putting their cases on them.

Penelope said: 'I still can't believe we're in Russia.'

'*I* can,' said Emily as the rest of the family clambered aboard with Mrs Hannay close behind.

The coach started off, moving slowly until it reached the highway. The snow at the side of the road looked as though it had been there for months.

There's nothing to worry about, Emily told herself; tourists can't get into trouble. She wondered whether she should tell Mrs Hannay as soon as they reached the hotel but decided to discuss it with Alyce first. Whichever course they chose, it looked as though the family's holiday in Russia might be more of an adventure than she had expected.

Three

❦

It had been their mother's idea, this trip to Russia. The children's enthusiasm had been a little forced but a holiday was a holiday even behind the Iron Curtain in the depths of winter. They were glad it was only for a week all the same; a week – they were sure – was long enough to see all the art treasures of Leningrad yet short enough to ensure that nothing serious went wrong. Russian 'flu would hardly have time to develop before they returned to the safety of England.

Emily viewed the seven days of museums and art galleries with some gloom; she preferred holidays in the outdoors where there were risks to take or wild places to be explored. The prospect of staying in a hotel was some compensation, however, because it was rare indeed for the family to afford such luxury and a hotel seemed to offer at least some opportunities for exploration. But now an unexpected source of adventure had presented itself. The very thought of it drew Emily's eyes away from the window to see where Mrs Hannay was sitting.

Mrs Hannay's fine, regular features must have been watching the back of Emily's head, for when Emily turned she found herself looking straight into the pale blue eyes.

Emily faced the front again wondering whether there was some message in that almost imperceptible movement of Mrs Hannay's head. Had Mrs Hannay seen the photograph too? Did she know that although the soldier had let her through she would be watched by the Soviet Police? For some time these questions absorbed Emily's attention to the exclusion of the dark winter landscape through which the coach was travelling. Eventually she decided that she would have to tell Alyce. Her instinct for survival suggested that the secret might be too dangerous to keep to herself. They would be sharing a room and at the first opportunity she would say to Alyce in a whisper (for the rooms might contain microphones), 'I think Mrs Hannay is being watched by the police.'

'They ate the people who died, didn't they?' a voice called from the centre of the coach.

Emily looked up sharply. Ilsa's description of the Siege of Leningrad in the Second World War had only touched the surface of Emily's attention. Behind Ilsa the main highway stretched broad and empty towards the lights of the city. On either side of the highway, the ground was flat and covered with snow.

'It was near this point,' Ilsa continued, not contradicting the voice but dismissing it with a smile that seemed to say she had heard that one before, 'that the Hitler armies were halted by heroic Russian soldiers and workers in September, 1941. The German Nazis besieged our city for nine hundred days. Over six thousand citizens died. The bread ration was 125 grams a day.'

'How much is that?' asked Shamus, evidently woken from his daydreams by the mention of food.

Ilsa replied: 'You know, 125 grams is about two or three slices.'

The passengers received this information in silence.

'When the Great Patriotic War was over,' Ilsa said after a while, 'Leningrad people rebuilt their city which had been almost completely destroyed by the Hitler armies. We are now approaching the Pavlovski District of our city. This is a new district and all the buildings you will see have been constructed after the end of the war.'

Emily was not sure what she had expected but from the first her impression of Russia was of the immense size of things. The highway was wider than any road she had seen; the blocks of flats in the Pavlovski District were probably no taller than those she had seen in London but they looked bigger because they seemed to rise so suddenly from the open landscape. When the coach passed the Moscow Gate and entered the older, central district of the city, Emily's feeling of being dwarfed by mighty buildings was even more pronounced for though the buildings themselves were not as tall as the blocks of flats they were much grander and made her feel small not only

in size but in importance. She could see no houses, at least nothing she would have called a house where she would have been happy to walk up to the front door and ring the bell. Every building looked like a palace (which indeed many of them had been once). There were magnificent fronts with white columns and coloured walls. There were great archways, high enough to take a double-decker bus, that led to courtyards. There were marble lions at the entrance.

A sense of awe in the face of such grandeur made the tourists lower their voices.

'Do people live here?' Alyce asked quietly, pointing towards the lighted windows of the palaces.

'The palaces of the nobility are now used by all the people,' Ilsa replied. 'They are offices, clubs for workers, hospitals and many other things.'

The coach passed along narrow streets, crossing and re-crossing the main thoroughfares of the city, on the way to the river. To the children's delight, the River Neva was covered with ice.

'Do you recognise it?' Emily heard Siobhan ask Mrs Hannay.

'The river?'

'No, everything.'

'It has not changed as much as I had expected,' said Mrs Hannay, 'but remember it is nearly sixty years since I left.'

'You must be very old, Mrs Hannay,' said Shamus.

Mrs Hannay said: 'I was seventeen when I left Russia. So what does that make me?'

'Eighty-seven,' replied Shamus, who preferred inspired guesswork to careful calculation.

'Seventy-seven,' Alyce corrected him at once.

'Where did you live, Mrs Hannay?' Emily asked.

They had crossed the river by the Troitsky Bridge and were travelling along the north bank towards their hotel. Mrs Hannay looked back across the ice to the buildings on the south bank.

'The long building with the statues on the roof,' she said, 'is the Winter Palace. We lived not far from there.'

Four

The Alexander Pushkin Hotel had been set at an angle to the river so that the rooms on the river side faced not only the former Winter Palace of Tsars but also the Admiralty with its slender gold spire which flashed like flame in the winter sunset. Despite its romantic name, the hotel was a plain modern block built to accommodate tourists and foreign delegations. It was close to the Peter and Paul Fortress, the first building of Peter the Great's city, and not far from the Finland Railway Station where Vladimir Ilych Lenin arrived in April 1917 to lead the Bolshevik Revolution.

These historical landmarks, so lovingly pointed out to the passengers by Ilsa, did not distract Emily from her thoughts about Mrs Hannay. Nor did she pay much attention to the successful outcome of her mother's plan. While the passengers from the first coach were being given keys to the rooms with odd numbers, Emily stood to one side of the queue thinking: has the soldier telephoned the police and have the police telephoned the hotel and is that man standing by the lift in a black suit that is too small for him a policeman in plain clothes?

'Your cases will be brought up to your rooms,' Ilsa informed them. 'Dinner is at eight o'clock and after dinner your Intourist representatives will give you your programme for tomorrow.'

'A programme, how awful!' groaned Siobhan, not loud enough for Ilsa to hear but drawing a sharp rebuke from her mother.

'Well it is awful,' Siobhan insisted as they moved towards the lifts. 'I hate being organised. Can't we ask Mrs Hannay to show us round?'

'I am sure she will, but we must go on the Intourist excursions as well. A lot has happened in sixty years.'

The lift shot upwards at alarming speed.

The family had been given four rooms on the eighth floor: three double rooms for the children and a single room for their mother. Emily shared with Alyce. The room was small with two beds placed end to end, fitted cupboards and, just inside the door on the right, a bathroom with a miniature bath in which not even Shamus or Jonathan would have been able to lie full length. A large plate glass window gave the widest possible view of the city.

'Bags this bed,' said Emily throwing her small case to claim the bed by the window.

Alyce said: 'You could walk across the ice to the Winter Palace. It has been known to freeze to a depth of two feet.'

'Who said?'

'It's a well-known fact.'

Emily jumped on to her bed and found it unexpectedly hard. Alyce's well-known facts were not well-known facts to anyone else. But despite all that information tucked away in her head and her unreasonable respect for the rules, Alyce could be a good ally and even adventurous at times if you caught her in the right mood. Emily decided that now was the right moment to tell Alyce about Mrs Hannay's photograph.

But Alyce was talking again, saying that someone called Rasputin had been pushed under the ice so that no one would find the body till the spring.

'Oriana's cat is called Rasputin,' Emily recalled.

'Oh, Emily, you're hopeless,' Alyce sighed wearily, 'Rasputin was a monk who was an evil influence on the last Tsar. Without him there might never have been a Revolution.'

'I think Russia's going to be exciting,' said Emily, hoping thus to lead on to the subject of Mrs Hannay.

'Interesting but not exciting,' said Alyce in a matter of fact tone. And she moved away from the window to unpack her neatly folded clothes and to place them carefully on the shelves in the cupboard.

Emily decided that the moment was not ripe after all. It was just as well for a few seconds later Shamus and Jonathan burst in. They were agog to find that they had their own bathroom and had come to see whether Alyce and Emily enjoyed the same privilege. They proposed a game of hide and seek.

'You go on, boys,' Emily told them, 'we'll meet you downstairs.'

'I know something about Mrs Hannay,' she added as soon as the door had closed.

'What?' Alyce had finished unpacking and was sliding her case underneath the bed.

'You know the soldier who checked our passports?'

'What about him?'

'He had a photograph of Mrs Hannay. I saw it when I learned over.'

Alyce made no comment but started to brush her long dark hair.

'He had lots of photographs,' Emily went on, 'they must be people who are wanted by the police.'

'Not necessarily.'

'Then why did he have their pictures to check?'

'Anyway,' said Alyce, ignoring the question, 'you must have made a mistake. They couldn't have a photograph of Mrs Hannay as she is now. She left Russia sixty years ago.'

Emily thrust out her jaw and closed her lips tightly. When she was angry or determined to have her way, her blue eyes glowed as though a small fire burned within.

'You'd better unpack your things,' said Alyce, 'it'll be dinner soon.'

Emily spoke through her teeth: 'I'll tell Mrs Hannay, then you'll believe me.'

The opportunity came at dinner. The members of the Intourist party sat together in one corner of the vast dining room at round tables for eight. As the family numbered seven, it was unanimously agreed that Mrs

Hannay should be invited to join them. She was travelling alone. She had already made their acquaintance. They did not imagine there was anything she would like better than to be admitted to their family circle. Like all large families they had a firm belief in the attractiveness of their own company.

Mrs Hannay declared that she would be delighted to join them. But Emily said nothing about the photograph. Alyce caught her eye from time to time but Emily only frowned. She did not, after all, wish to share her secret with the whole family. There was one thing that Mrs Hannay said about herself, however (or at least one thing that she did not exactly deny) that even Alyce had to agree tended to support Emily's suspicion that the Russian police were interested in keeping an eye on this elderly lady who was returning to her homeland for the first time in sixty years.

The meal was plain: hot vegetable soup, salted fish served cold, brown rye bread, cake and fruit. Each table had four bottles of apple juice to share among the guests. On the far side of the dining-room, with their backs to the windows that looked out on the dark river, the members of a small band were playing music of a curiously indefinite sort – neither Russian folk music nor Western pop but an unsatisfying blend of the two.

Mrs Hannay was quizzed by the children about the city as it used to be before the Revolution. Her brief factual answers were so tantalising, so evocative of a different world, that Emily could not help saying: 'It must be so funny, coming back again.'

Mrs Hannay smiled at her. 'Do you remember the building on the right by the canal? Ilsa pointed it out to us when the coach stopped before crossing Nevsky Prospekt. The chandeliers were alight in the ballroom on the first floor just as they used to be. It was as if nothing had changed.'

'Ballroom!' exclaimed Emily. 'Only hotels have ballrooms.'

'And palaces,' Alyce corrected her.

'It was the Stroganov Palace,' Mrs Hannay confirmed, 'we went there often as children.'

'Were you a princess, Mrs Hannay?' Emily asked.

To which Mrs Hannay gave a rather vague reply.

'We all had absurd titles in those days,' she said.

Five

❧

'Isn't it lucky that Mrs Hannay is on this trip.'

Emily's thought was evidently shared by the other members of the family. They were occupying a settee and two arm chairs in one corner of the hotel lounge. The twins had disappeared, restless to explore further before bedtime. Mrs Hannay had gone to her room.

'Perhaps she is a princess,' Penelope speculated.

'Then she has a nerve to come back,' declared Siobhan.

'Why do you think she has come back, Mummy?' Emily asked.

'I expect she wants to see all the places she knew when she was young. She might have relatives here still. Had you thought of that?'

'I'm surprised they allowed her in,' said Siobhan, at which Emily glanced at Alyce but said nothing.

'Why shouldn't they?' Penelope appeared to find Siobhan's attitude provocative. 'The Revolution was a long time ago.'

'The rich are always guilty,' Siobhan intoned.

'Well, Siobhan, you tell us something about the Revolution,' said her mother quickly, 'and you too, Penelope, you've been doing it at school, I know.'

Normally the girls would have been most reluctant to respond to such a request, but on this occasion Siobhan and Penelope rose keenly to the challenge.

'There were *two* Revolutions,' Penelope began, 'both here in St Petersburg and both in 1917, one in February and one in October.'

'The October Revolution was the important one,' Siobhan pointed out.

'They were both important,' Penelope disagreed, 'the first one overthrew the Tsar's rule and the second one brought Lenin to power.'

'All right, they were both important,' Siobhan cut in impatiently, 'but it isn't the facts of history that matter, it's the reason why. For hundreds of years the rich nobles, people like Mrs Hannay's family I expect, lived in luxury while millions of ordinary people starved. The only surprising thing is that the Revolution didn't start earlier.'

'But what happened?' Emily demanded. She was not interested in the reasons why; history was an adventure to be relived, though you would never have thought so from the way Miss Bigenshaw taught it at school.

'What happened,' said Siobhan with the air of someone providing the final and complete answer, 'was that the "haves" were thrown out and the "have-nots" were given a chance for the first time in Russian history.'

'What happened,' said Penelope, 'was that one cruel ruler was replaced by another.'

'That is *not* what happened!'

'Siobhan darling there's no need to shout.'

'Mummy, you don't understand,' said Siobhan, lowering her voice nevertheless.

'How can we understand,' Emily protested, 'when you are arguing the whole time?'

'It's quite simple,' Siobhan insisted, 'the people, the real people, that is, not the Royal Family and their aristocratic friends, seized power because they were not prepared to be treated like animals any longer.'

'They murdered the Royal Family,' Penelope pointed out quietly.

'Why not? They were responsible for the deaths of hundreds of workers.'

'The children weren't. Nothing makes it right to murder children.'

Siobhan raised her eyes to the ceiling as if to say, 'What is the use of arguing with someone who misses the point?' and sank back on the sofa with a sigh.

'Well,' said their mother after a pause, 'no one can say this isn't an interesting city. Didn't Ilsa tell us that that warship opposite the hotel was the one that fired a blank shot as a signal for the Revolution?'

Penelope nodded. 'For the storming of the Winter Palace.'

But interest in the Revolution had run out for the moment and conversation drifted on to less controversial topics such as the time of breakfast and whether Daddy would have remembered to give the cat her evening meal.

The twins returned and announced that there were shops in the hotel and another restaurant on the top floor. These discoveries so proudly presented were received in silence.

'Time you two were in bed,' said their mother, 'you're all very tired.'

'We're not,' said Shamus, his face pale with the long drawn out excitement of the day, 'are we, Johnny?'

Jonathan puckered his heavily freckled face and shook his head slowly. It was clear that if he did not go to bed soon he would fall asleep standing up.

The four girls were left on their own. Other guests moved in and out of the lounge. The hotel appeared to be full for no sooner had one group vacated their chairs than another moved in to occupy the same seats. Outside the enormous windows that reached from floor to ceiling it was just possible to make out the shape of the cruiser *Aurora* whose gun had fired the shot on that October night in 1917.

'Do you think Mrs Hannay's family were murdered?' Emily asked Penelope.

'I doubt it,' Penelope replied, 'the family probably escaped altogether.'

'It's a bit risky coming back then,' Emily said.

Six

Alyce was still asleep. Emily knelt at the end of her own bed and drew aside the curtain. Darkness and snow. The snow was falling out of the darkness. The people of Leningrad were going to work. A single-decker bus ran past the hotel and turned slowly on to the Troitsky Bridge. On the pavements and the forecourt of the hotel women were clearing the snow using shovels with enormous wooden blades. The women wore rough clothes and aprons of sacking. The snowflakes settled on their head scarves and on their shoulders. The men who hurried along the pavements carrying brief cases and, thickly wrapped against the cold, did not appear to give the women a second thought.

Emily's eye rested on the street lamps set in the stone embankment wall. Each iron stem held four arms like a giant candelabra. From these yellow lights her eye moved on to the vast frozen surface of the River Neva. As far as the morning darkness would allow she traced the route she would take if she was forced to cross the ice escaping from the Revolutionaries. She could see that the ice was not solid from bank to bank but formed large floating islands separated by narrow channels of pitch-black water. The snow made it more difficult to see where these channels were and to try to cross the river now would be a hazardous undertaking. What hope of survival would you have, Emily wondered, if you slipped when jumping from one island to the next? Even if the freezing water didn't knock you unconscious you might be trapped under the ice. And when at last you found the surface and the open air, the side of the ice island would not be firm like the side of a swimming pool: it would tilt under your weight so that for all your kicking you would slide back into the darkness. They would find your body in the spring when the ice melted.

'Breakfast is served in the main dining-room on the ground floor,' Alyce's business-like voice announced from the river bank as Emily went down for the last time.

Alyce was sitting up in bed, her dark hair resting on the front of her shoulders.

Emily rolled back on to the rumpled bedclothes hoping to recapture the exact position of warmth and cosiness she had left a few moments earlier. But Alyce was up now and setting about the business of dressing for the morning's expedition with such brisk efficiency, it was impossible to lie still in the same room.

Emily sprang out of bed with forced gusto.

'We'd better get on the same coach as Mrs Hannay,' she said.

The two Intourist coaches left the hotel forecourt at ten o'clock sharp. Emily pressed Mrs Hannay to join the family. There was no doubt that theirs was the better coach. Not only was Ilsa their guide but she was accompanied by a colleague called Mr Oblamov. He had been standing near the coaches watching the tourists sort themselves into two groups before climbing aboard himself. He sat in the swivel seat next to the driver and when Ilsa introduced him to the passengers, he stood, nodded his head to left and right as though acknowledging discreet applause and then sat down again. He was not what Emily would have called a typical Russian but a small man with soft, almost feminine features. He had chestnut coloured hair and large brown eyes. In the lapel of his overcoat was a small red badge with a profile of Lenin. He held his fur hat in his hands.

Ilsa told the passengers that Mr Oblamov was the Leningrad Secretary of Intourist; he had chosen to join this tour in order to assure himself and his committee that the representatives of the British people enjoyed their visit to 'our city'. He would be pleased to hear the suggestions of his British friends for the improvement of the arrangements that had been made. In the meantime, on behalf of the Board of Tourism for the Council of Ministers of the Soviet Union, he wished everyone a pleasant holiday.

Flattered that he should choose their coach, the passengers settled down to enjoy the tour of the city.

The morning turned out well. It stopped snowing and as the day brightened and the sky cleared the buildings that had appeared drab emerged in their full glory. It had been the custom for two hundred years to paint the outside of the most important buildings in colour: sage-green, rose, emerald, turquoise-blue and yellow. The colour was painted on the flat surface so that it contrasted with the white of the pillars and the bright gold of the mouldings. On a grey day these painted surfaces, far from adding colour to the northern city, only served to emphasise how bleak it was, but when the sun touched the colours, particularly the winter sun that dropped early in the afternoon casting long, slanting rays of gold over the city, the buildings came to life. In this sunlight the painted surfaces appeared warm and rich: the drab buildings became splendid palaces and the bleak northern city was transformed into a place of grandeur and magnificence.

The coach tour took two hours. From the window Emily watched the famous landmarks go by – the Peter and Paul Fortress, the Winter Palace, the bronze statue of Peter the Great, the Kazan Cathedral – enjoying the warm laziness of it all. Ilsa explained the history and significance of each landmark and the coach stopped for a few minutes for the passengers to take photographs. Occasionally a piece of history interested Emily – especially the long siege by the Germans in the Great Patriotic War because she could imagine herself hurrying along these streets while the bombs fell and queueing at this corner for the daily ration of bread – but she preferred to watch the Russian people. It was the school holidays and there were many children shopping with their parents. The large shops on Nevsky Prospekt had Christmas decorations in the window. Ilsa explained that on the Russian calendar tomorrow was Christmas Day.

'But you don't have Christmas any more!' Siobhan exclaimed.

Ilsa glanced at Mr Oblamov. 'Christmas is not a religious festival for Russian people,' she said, 'only the old people go to church now.'

While Siobhan sat back with an air of satisfaction, Alyce asked whether some of the old people would still remember what it was like in Russia before the Revolution. It was Mr Oblamov who replied. He had spun slowly in his seat and was facing the passengers. He said: 'There are a few people of the older generation who would remember. In our country these people are treated with respect because they have known the long struggle for Socialism. In our country there is no conflict between old and young: every generation has something to learn from the others.'

This sentiment drew murmurs of approval from the passengers, but Alyce cut across them, saying: 'Would you let one of the old nobility come back then?'

This question did not find favour with the other passengers. 'You shouldn't ask that,' said a female voice and two or three other voices called, 'Hear, hear.'

The coach was travelling along Maierova Prospekt towards the great marble columns and golden dome of St Isaac's Cathedral. As the coach slowed down to park in Cathedral Square, Mr Oblamov spread his arms wide in a gesture that seemed to suggest tolerance and unlimited goodwill.

'The Soviet Union welcomes all people,' he replied to Alyce, 'as long as they come in a spirit of friendship.'

There was a brief round of applause. His finely balanced features broke into a smile, revealing perfect small, white teeth. The passengers responded with smiles of their own. If all Russians were like Mr Oblamov, the mood of the passengers seemed to say, there would always be friendship between our two countries.

The coach stopped. The passengers got out to take photographs. Emily sat tight and frowned. Mr Oblamov's reply to Alyce had done nothing to support her theory that Mrs Hannay was an unwelcome visitor. It could have been a lie of course. She looked furtively at Mr Oblamov who, like Ilsa and the driver, had remained in the coach. Ilsa smiled. The building opposite the Cathedral, she told Emily, was the seat of the Executive Committee of the Leningrad City Soviet. Emily thought she had never heard of anything so dull. The dark grey stone seemed to echo her mood of depression. If Mrs Hannay was not being watched by the police, what else was there to do in Russia?

The passengers moved about the square seeking better shots of the Cathedral or stood in groups stamping their feet and smacking their gloved hands against the cold. Emily watched them gloomily. This was not the stuff of which adventures were made. In the background she could hear Mr Oblamov and Ilsa talking in Russian and the driver humming to himself. If only she had remained at home she could have had Oriana to stay. Now the last week of the holidays would be used up trudging round museums or standing in the freezing air looking at palaces that weren't palaces any more.

She became aware that Mr Oblamov and Ilsa had stopped talking and she turned to see what had attracted their attention. Ilsa had got up to open the coach door for the returning passengers but Mr Oblamov was staring intently out of the front window across the square. Following the direction of his gaze, she saw Mrs Hannay talking to a Russian woman, younger and more strongly built than herself; she had evidently stopped a passer-by to ask a direction for the woman was pointing to a narrow street that led from the square.

Emily glanced at Mr Oblamov's face. Though she could see only this side of his head it was enough. His expression was quite different from that of a tourist guide who fears that one of his party may keep the coach waiting. He was watching Mrs Hannay with the absolute attention of a policeman watching a burglar or a hunter watching his prey.

Seven

❧

It was one of their mother's characteristics that she wanted to go to places that were not on the programme and to do things for which no arrangements had been made. This desire to go one better was embarrassing enough at home where shopkeepers were asked to make a special reduction and visitors to the house were pressed into one domestic task or another, but this was nothing to the embarrassment that the children felt here in a foreign country when their mother decided that she would like to attend a church service on the Russian Christmas Day. What made it worse in their eyes was that she had persuaded Mrs Hannay to do the asking.

'You can't possibly go this morning,' Siobhan protested, 'we are due to visit the Russian State Museum.'

'We can go there another day.'

'Mr Oblamov may be offended,' Penelope murmured.

'I'm sure he'd understand. He did ask for suggestions, don't forget.'

'Then you should have asked him yourself,' said Alyce.

Their mother cheerfully brushed aside these criticisms. Mrs Hannay had been brought up in the Russian Orthodox Church; it was natural that she should approach Mr Oblamov.

A few minutes later Mr Oblamov appeared among them suddenly, as though they had unintentionally spoken a magic word. Emily was to note as the days went by that he had a knack of just being there without anyone having seen him approach, a curious talent for a man who claimed to be responsible for tourism.

'Your friend Mrs Hannay has told me of your request,' he said, 'I shall be happy to accompany you to St Basil's Church myself . . .'

'Oh, there's no need,' their mother protested.

'There's no need but I should like to do so,' he said solemnly. 'The constitution of our country gives to every citizen freedom of religious opinion. There are three churches in Leningrad where services will be held today. With your permission I shall take you to St Basil's. It is the principal Christian church in our city.'

'That is very kind of you,' said their mother, 'but I am sure Mrs Hannay and I can find our way.'

'I have arranged for a car,' Mr Oblamov continued as though she had not spoken, 'it will be here at ten o'clock. And the children: do they wish to come?'

'I'm going to the Russian State Museum,' Siobhan announced, 'Shamus and Jonathan can come with me.'

Penelope opted for St Basil's.

Emily touched Alyce's arm.

'Let's go to church,' she proposed.

That Emily should wish to attend a church service of her own free will was so unexpected that Alyce did not immediately understand. Emily raised her eyebrows to signify that there was a good reason.

'What is it?' Alyce asked impatiently when Mr Oblamov had gone and Emily had drawn her aside in a conspiratorial manner.

It was the day after their tour of the city. Last night Alyce had refused to accept that Mr Oblamov was a policeman in plain clothes just because he had been watching Mrs Hannay talking to a passer-by in Cathedral Square.

'You didn't see the look on his face,' Emily had retorted.

But now Emily could say with triumph, 'I told you he was a policeman.'

'Not that again,' sighed Alyce, glancing round the hotel foyer as though seeking a more interesting topic.

'Then why is he taking us to the church himself,' hissed Emily, 'when he could have let us go alone in a taxi. It's because he's been told not to let Mrs Hannay out of his sight, that's why.'

Alyce shrugged this new evidence away but without the absolute assurance of the night before. And she did agree that it might be interesting for one or other of them to watch Mr Oblamov the whole day, both on the morning's visit to the church and during their first visit to the Winter Palace in the afternoon. It should not be too difficult to tell whether he was spying on Mrs Hannay.

The large black car sped through the streets of Leningrad. It was just another working day for the people of the city, no concession being made to the minority who celebrated the birth of Christ on this day. Mr Oblamov sat in the front, leaving the three children, their mother and Mrs Hannay to squeeze on to the back seat. Unlike Ilsa, Mr Oblamov made no comment on the buildings and squares they passed, his only sign of interest in the journey being brief instructions to the driver. At the back of his head (Emily noted with satisfaction) his chestnut hair was cut in a neat horizontal line, military fashion.

St Basil's Church possessed neither the monumental grandeur of St Isaac's Cathedral nor the colourful decoration of the eighteenth century churches Ilsa had shown them on the city tour. It was large and white and rather ugly like a huge blancmange topped with three golden onion shaped towers that caught the morning sun. The church stood in the centre of what appeared to be a small park, for there were swings and a slide where children were playing. The top of the slide was about eight feet from the ground and was reached by a steep, narrow flight of steps. Water had been poured down the wood so that the surface was a layer of hard ice. The children slid down on the soles of their shoes, crouching with legs full bent and hands thrust forward to keep a balance. When they reached the bottom of the slide they whizzed several yards further over the tight-packed snow. As the tourists approached, one or two of the older boys (Emily put them at thirteen or so) came forward holding dirty one ruble notes in their red fingers, but Mr Oblamov sent them packing with a sharp phrase.

'What did they want?' Penelope asked.

'It is against the law,' was Mr Oblamov's reply.

'Will they get into trouble?'

'Not this time. They are lucky.'

Because you can't arrest them now, Emily thought, without showing yourself to be a policeman. But when they realised who you were they ran fast enough.

Mr Oblamov led the way into the church. They passed through a door cut out of a much larger door, wooden and massive, filling the great arch at the west end of the building. Inside there was no daylight and it took some time for Emily's eyes to adjust to the pattern of candlelight and shadow. She could not at first make out what was going on. There were no seats. If there was a service in progress it was a very informal one for the crowd of people was constantly on the move, murmuring as it went. On the walls and pillars were paintings on wood of men with fierce faces and staring eyes. The paintings were lit by candles.

'Aren't the icons wonderful?' her mother whispered in her ear.

Emily nodded though 'wonderful' was not the word she would have chosen. Each icon was covered with a sheet of glass. The worshippers kissed the glass in front of the icon and then wiped the place clean with a cloth that hung at the side. The authorities insisted on the glass, Mr Oblamov told them on the way home, the icons being more likely to spread disease than perform miracles.

Emily decided that kissing icons was definitely not her style. She went to church when she had to and sang when she liked the hymn tune but kissing things was foreign and odd. She stood firmly in one place refusing to be drawn towards an icon where some action might be expected of her.

Mr Oblamov made enquiries of a young, bearded priest and then beckoned his party to follow him to the far end of the church where a spiral staircase was just visible in the shadows. The actual service was being held upstairs, he informed them, looking a bit put out that he had not known this at the start. 'I will wait for you in the car,' he added, glancing round at the religious devotion with distaste.

'We would not want you to wait,' said Mrs Hannay softly, 'I think I noticed that the tram outsides goes to the Finland Station. That is close to our hotel, is it not?'

Once again, Mr Oblamov appeared to ignore a suggestion that did not fit in with his programme. 'I will wait in the car,' he repeated.

It was clear to Emily that he had his orders and that he would not dare depart from them.

She said: 'I don't think I'll come upstairs, Mummy. I feel rather funny.' She did her best to look pale. 'I'll stay outside and get some fresh air. I'd like to try the slide.'

Her mother hesitated and then agreed. 'But keep warm whatever you do. It's much colder than you realise. She can sit in the car if she feels cold, can't she, Mr Oblamov?'

'Certainly,' he replied without effort.

When the others had disappeared upwards into the dark, Mr Oblamov said to Emily: 'So, I shall wait in the car. You remember where it is parked?'

'Yes, thank you.'

She was relieved that he chose to go ahead, thrusting his way through the crowd with little ceremony like a colonial policeman in a native bazaar. 'So much mumbo-jumbo,' his quick steps and bobbing fur hat seemed to say.

Outside, the Russian children eyed Emily's expensive winter clothes and Emily returned their gaze with a steady, open look. With her fair hair and skin, her deep blue eyes and her sturdy frame Emily might have been Russian herself, or at least from one of those provinces on the Baltic Sea that the Russians have always swallowed up at the first opportunity. Certainly she did not look out of place among the children who now welcomed her into their game.

A girl of about Emily's age, with a pale, lively face beneath a woollen, egg-warmer hat, invited Emily to follow her up the steps to the top of the slide.

'Do you speak English?' Emily asked as they mounted the steps.

At the top, the girl turned, shook her head and smiled.

Then, before Emily had a chance to see how it was done, she crouched down and shot forward at great speed, maintaining her balance with the apparent ease of long practice.

Emily watched from the top step. There was no platform so she would have to take her position on the icy slope by gripping the wooden sides with both hands. It was nothing like as easy as it had appeared from below. To give herself time, she looked down the course to the snow bank among the trees that acted as a buffer to prevent you careering into the railings that divided the park from the street. Beyond the railings two men were standing on the pavement, talking. One was Mr Oblamov. The other was a much larger, burlier man in the long grey greatcoat and grey fur hat that Emily had seen several times on the streets of Leningrad. He was either a policeman or an army officer, she was not sure which. She smiled to herself. If further proof was needed of Mr Oblamov's real identity, this was it. Their holiday in Russia was not going to be just a dull trudge from museum to museum. It was going to be an adventure in which she would play the leading part.

With a surge of bravado, she gripped the wooden sides in her gloved hands, placed her boots on the hard ice and then, crouching low, pushed her head and shoulders as far forward over her knees as she dared. Below, all the Russian children had stopped to watch her. She was nervous and happy. This was what life was about, not exams or homework or silly rules that teachers made up for their own protection, but risks and adventure, the thrill of being afraid and the joy of meeting fear head on and conquering.

She let go her grip and put her arms forward. The speed of the descent startled her as she hurtled down the narrow slope. She realised that she had no idea how to cope with the sudden change of angle when she hit the ground. At the bottom of the slide her feet shot forward away from her and her body sprawled back on to the hard-packed snow. The impact winded her momentarily and she struggled for breath. In this undignified position she whizzed along the surface until her feet hit the buffer. There she lay, gasping and laughing with excitement and relief. She could hear the cries of the Russian children as they ran towards her. She looked up at the trees where the snow was lodged in the joints. Above the branches the sky was as clear and blue as on a summer's day.

Eight

❧

In the early afternoon the sun was already going down the sky and its golden light fell across the south face of the Winter Palace. Even Emily (who found other people's enthusiasm for the buildings of Leningrad a little tiresome) was stunned by the size and colour of the Palace. This south face must have been all of 150 yards long and looked even longer for it had only a ground floor and two storeys. The white and gold decoration set against the sage-green stucco on the walls glowed rich and warm in the slanting sunlight. It was eleven degrees below freezing point but the Palace seemed to be basking in the soft, mellow light of a summer evening.

The coach had parked in Palace Square. As the passengers dismounted, a squad of cadets from the Leningrad Naval Academy marched by, and Siobhan could not resist comparing these young men favourably with the 'drop-outs and hooligans in England'. Emily was not so impressed. The boys (for they did not look older than sixteen) were smart enough but their expressions were utterly serious as though they could never take a joke or see the funny side of things.

The passengers followed the cadets towards the river and the north face of the Palace. As they passed from the sunlight into the shadow of the building they felt the full impact of the cold. Despite the temperature a long queue of Russian people waited patiently for admission to the Palace. The queue stretched from the Main Entrance in

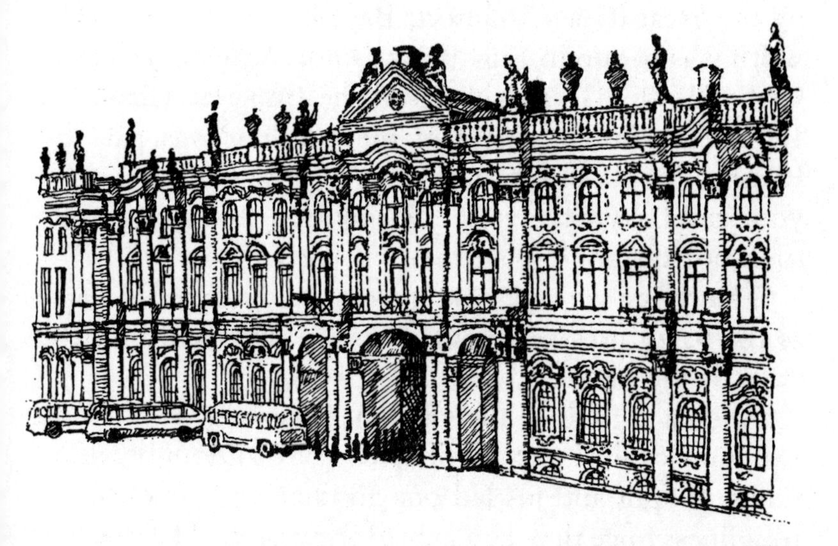

the centre of the north face right round the building to the edge of the Square. Tourists were allowed to jump the queue, a privilege that Siobhan declared she did not wish to enjoy but would do so in order not to cause difficulties for Ilsa. Emily shadowed Mr Oblamov. She had agreed to take the first hour or their two hour tour of the Palace; at half past three on the dot, she would hand over to Alyce.

Near the head of the queue a man was selling hot doughnuts from a stall and was doing a good trade. Immediately behind him – and he might have chosen his position with an eye to this visual aid – was one of the giant drainpipes on the Palace wall from whose wide mouth a broad tongue of ice hung down onto the pavement.

'We are now going to enter the Winter Palace,' Ilsa told them, 'where you may see the collection of paintings and other treasures that belong to the State Hermitage Museum. The Palace was built for the Tsarina Elizabeth by the great Italian architect, Bartolemeo Rastrelli. The work was begun in 1754 but was not finished until after Catherine the Great had seized the Imperial Throne in 1763. The immense cost of the building was paid by Russian people through new taxes on salt and wine. So you could say that, at the Revolution, Russian people took possession of their own property.'

'That's one way of looking at it,' said a cheerful voice as the party pressed forward up the steps and into the door of the Palace.

Inside it was all confusion. The Russians, who would wait outside for hours in the bitter cold without breaking ranks, fought and jostled one another with astonishing roughness once they had gained admission. The cause of this rough-house was the rule (common to all Russian museums and theatres) that overcoats and hats had to be checked in at the cloakroom. As the latter was quite inadequate to handle the number of visitors arriving at one time, let alone those who were departing, the need to adopt an attitude of every man for himself was at once apparent. Ilsa apologised but could do nothing. Mr Oblamov frowned, his slight stature and gentle manners being ill-suited to the rough-and-tumble. But for Emily the struggle to hand in coat and fur hat provided a new challenge, not of nerve as the slide had done that morning, but of physical determination and ingenuity. She plunged into the swaying, jostling throng.

It was quickly brought home to her that the Russian women were more to be feared as opponents than the men; they fought harder (indeed they actually seemed stronger) and used their feet and elbows with complete disregard for the feelings of those who stood in their way. Emily's technique was a combination of toughness and cunning. She was strong enough to push herself through any half-opening and when her way was blocked she would say, 'Excuse me!' in English, the strange tongue and child's voice being just enough to cause the Russian people to turn and leave a gap through which she could wriggle.

Even when you succeeded in reaching the front, there was no guarantee that your coat and hat would be taken. The only attendant was a grey old man with a cunning expression and sharp yellow eyes. He clearly relished the power his position gave him. He chose to take some coats and refuse others. Visitors who pleaded with him were ignored; those who cursed him were kept waiting all the longer. Emily summed up the situation quickly enough. She stuffed her fur hat into the pocket of her overcoat, rolled the coat into a ball and threw it at the attendant striking him full on the chest.

'Thank you,' she said politely, reaching out to take the small metal disc that his hand had placed involuntarily on the counter.

She heard his hoarse shout as she turned and disappeared back into the throng, twisting this way and that to make a passage.

The other members of Ilsa's party did not find the business of handing in their coats so challenging, though young Jonathan made a good showing for a boy of his size. The adults, looking rather battered, rallied round Ilsa as though she was their standard bearer and it was necessary to check how many had fallen in the fray. But when they all moved forward, the dazzling white marble and beautiful mirrors on the grand staircase soon soothed the ruffled tempers.

They entered a treasure-house of overwhelming richness and variety. One lofty chamber led to another until it seemed that there would never be an end to the procession of graceful rooms. Each room was devoted to an aspect of the treasure: silver, armour, costume, precious stones, furniture, above all paintings. The Romanov Tsars and their wealthy nobles had been enthusiastic collectors. There were more than four thousand paintings, Ilsa informed them. 'All the great masters are represented here,' she added with pride.

Ilsa guided her party from one genius to the next: in this room Rembrandt, in this Tintoretto, in this Van Dyck, in this Velasquez, in this Rubens, each master represented not by one or two paintings but by four walls covered with his creations. Late in the tour the party came to a room overlooking the River Neva and with an audible expression of relief the tourists turned away from the paintings to look out at the frozen river and the winter sky.

'Look at the sun! Look at the sun,' cried Shamus pointing to the golden spire of the Cathedral of St Peter and St Paul.

'Who are these by?' Penelope asked Ilsa, seeing that their guide was standing alone.

'Raphael,' Ilsa replied, 'they are all by Raphael.'

If such a surfeit of genius had been too much for the adults, the younger children had long since lost interest. Their mother had continued to point out paintings of special interest – for was this not the reason she had brought them to Leningrad – but their responses had become less and less enthusiastic.

'Look dears, this is Kneller's portrait of John Locke.'

'He looks so old,' Shamus had said, yawning and letting his tired eyes drift away on to the fire extinguisher in the corner.

'Is this the last room,' Jonathan had asked, tapping his knuckles on the statue of Voltaire to see if it was hollow.

As soon as Emily's hour was up she handed over to Alyce, whispering as she did so that she had noticed nothing suspicious in Mr Oblamov's behaviour. Then she retired to the back of the group, casting about for some opportunity to draw excitement from the remainder of the tour. She noticed that in some of the rooms there were doors that were kept closed, presumably leading to those sections of the Palace not open to the public. Bored by the pictures, she allowed her imagination to create the scene behind those locked doors: they were the Royal Apartments which the modern Russians were never permitted to see; the rooms had not been touched since the Revolution so that the chairs and tables, the curtains and carpets (and the dead bodies of the courtiers?) were covered with a thick layer of dust.

She would have liked to try one of the doors but in every room there was a woman on duty, dressed in black and sitting on a chair. There was no time to wait and see whether the women ever moved, but Emily decided that she would come back on one of the free afternoons at the end of the visit. On her own – or with Alyce to look out – she was sure she could find a way to slip unnoticed into the forbidden rooms.

The tour of the Winter Palace neared its conclusion. Ilsa asked her party to give special attention to the last picture she would show them. With the reserve of energy that can always be found for the final lap, the tourists approached the picture with light, brisk steps. It was not attached to the wall but set on a stand in the centre of the room.

Emily found herself near the front of the loose semicircle that formed. The picture did not look much: a Virgin Mary and Baby Jesus. She seemed to have seen half a dozen like it in the last two hours. She looked round to see where Alyce and Mr Oblamov had got to. They were standing side by side. Alyce made a face that could have meant anything from 'Nothing to report' to 'I've solved the mystery'. She really had no talent for undercover work. Emily mouthed 'What?' and frowned, but her attention was drawn to Mr Oblamov who was showing a keen interest in the painting. If he is what he says he is, she thought, he will have seen this painting hundreds of times before, so why is he looking at it so keenly and listening so carefully to every word that Ilsa is saying.

'This painting of the Madonna and Child is the most valuable in the collection,' Ilsa told them. 'It is by the Italian master, Leonardo da Vinci. The painting was brought to Russia in the nineteenth century by a group of Italian actors who did not know its true value. They sold it to a Russian nobleman, Prince Nicolai Dubinsky who recognised that it was a Leonardo. In 1917, the Tsar Nicholas II agreed to buy the painting from the Dubinsky family for the Hermitage Museum for one million rubles; but only one instalment of 100,000 rubles had been paid when the Great October Socialist Revolution occurred and the painting became the property of the world's first Government of Workers and Peasants. So now all Russian people can see this masterpiece because it is the policy in our country that works of art belong to the people.'

Emily looked at the Leonardo with new interest. If it had been worth a million rubles in 1917 and there were one and a half rubles to the pound . . . But the mathematics was too much of a burden at the end of a long day. It was a surprisingly small picture to be so valuable, no bigger than a foolscap exercise book. An odd painting too: the Madonna looked much too young to have a baby and the Child Jesus, sitting naked on his mother's knee, was rather fat and had a bald head that appeared too large for the rest of his body.

Someone asked whether the Dubinsky family had ever claimed the painting back since the whole sum had not been paid and this drew a round of tired, unsympathetic laughter. The tourists were all too weary, too richly overfed with the masterpieces of the past to care about the rights and wrongs of ownership. Understanding this, Ilsa smiled and did not answer the question.

In twos and threes the party descended the grand staircase to reclaim their coats and hats. Shamus and Jonathan, as eager to leave as they had been to come, dodged in and out. Innocently, Emily gave her disc to Siobhan with the request that she should collect her coat as well while she was about it. Then she seized Alyce's arm.

'What did you mean back there?' she demanded, drawing Alyce into an alcove where the head and shoulders of a Roman general stood on a black marble pedestal.

'I've decided you're right,' Alyce replied simply.

Emily could not imagine what clue Alyce had discovered in Mr Oblamov's behaviour that afternoon that had convinced her of his real identity. But it was not about Mr Oblamov that Alyce spoke.

She said: 'Remember when you told me about the photograph of Mrs Hannay, the one you saw on the soldier's desk at the airport? Well, I didn't believe you because I couldn't see how they could have an up-to-date photograph of her.'

'They did have,' said Emily, unsure where all this was leading.

'Right, and you know how they got it?'

'How?'

'It's her visa photograph. We all had to give in two when we applied for a visa to enter Russia. So of course it was easy for them to have an up-to-date one of Mrs Hannay.'

'But why was it on the soldier's desk?' said Emily, resisting the temptation to say I told you so. 'And what about Mr Oblamov? Why is he watching her so closely?'

'I don't know,' Alyce confessed. 'If Mr Oblamov is a policeman . . .'

'He is,' Emily assured her.

'All right, let's say he is. It may be just because she was born here and nothing more than that.'

'That isn't enough,' Emily argued, 'it has to be something she did or something she was. That's why they are suspicious of her.'

Nine

Emily thought that they might solve the mystery of Mrs Hannay by persuading her to talk about her childhood, for if there was a clue to her importance to the present Russian authorities it must surely lie in those years before the Revolution. It was unlikely, to say the least, that Mrs Hannay was an English spy but it was just possible that she was carrying messages to people in Leningrad.

'No,' said Alyce, 'you were right the first time. It is something in the past.'

They tackled Mrs Hannay at supper. The opportunity came because their mother had taken Siobhan and Penelope to the Kirov Ballet (the one official visit in two days' time being enough for Alyce and Emily) and the twins were already in bed, flat out after the long afternoon in the Winter Palace.

'Did you ever go to the Winter Palace in the old days?' Emily asked.

Mrs Hannay seemed to be in no hurry to answer the question. She cut her apple into four sections and then carefully removed the pips from each. Emily, who was not accustomed to pauses in the conversation, asked again.

'Just once,' Mrs Hannay replied, 'today was the second time in sixty years.'

She smiled at the thought, but if the girls thought that this was a preliminary to a description of that first visit they were disappointed. Mrs Hannay talked about the city before the Revolution, about the life she had led as a child, the winters in the city and the summers at their estate near the Baltic coast, and she neatly side-stepped Emily's attempts to bring her back to the point. The conversation turned to Mrs Hannay's family.

'My father was a soldier,' Mrs Hannay told them.

'Was he a general?' Alyce asked.

'He was killed by his own men,' was Mrs Hannay's way of replying.

'Because he was a general?'

'Yes. Lenin sent an order that all officers were to stop fighting against the Germans. My father refused. They lynched him, his own men, led by his own second-in-command, Bazorov.'

'How horrible!' Emily exclaimed. She did not know exactly what 'lynched' meant but it sounded unpleasant enough.

'That was how things were in 1917.'

'What happened to you?' Alyce asked.

'We escaped – my mother, my sister Katherine and I – it is a long story. We were in Finland and then in Paris. We had a little money, a few jewels disguised as buttons on our coats, but not enough. My mother took a job with a music publisher. We all spoke French of course, because in St Petersburg the nobility spoke nothing else; some of our friends couldn't even speak Russian though our father insisted that we learnt it. He loved his country very dearly. In Paris my sister and I studied at the Sorbonne. If it had not been for the death of our dear father the Revolution could be said to have done us good. We had to stand on our feet for the first time in our lives. In Petersburg we had been terribly spoilt: ten servants living in, a personal maid to brush my hair every night and two butlers to serve at table. It was another world.'

'Sounds all right,' said Emily.

The waiter poured Mrs Hannay's coffee.

'I don't think you would have liked it,' she told Emily.

'Yes I would. I wouldn't have had to make my bed every morning.'

Mrs Hannay laughed. 'We were too rich all the same. No one needs to be that rich.'

'What happened to all your things?' Alyce asked.

'We left them behind; apart from the jewels of course. The museums have some; my father was a great collector.'

Alyce, who was a great believer in private property and who had a notice on her bedroom door which read "Everything in this room belongs to Alyce", said: 'I should hate to see my precious things in a museum.'

'You haven't got any,' said Emily.

'Yes, but if I had.'

'You don't have to own things to appreciate their beauty,' said Mrs Hannay.

A second waiter, this one in a bottle green jacket, approached the table wishing to clear away, but Emily was determined to have an answer to her original question. When had Mrs Hannay gone to the Winter Palace?

'I went with my father,' Mrs Hannay replied, in no way put out by Emily's insistence, 'not long before the first Revolution when Mr Kerensky came to power, so it must have been in the winter of 1916. My father had some business with a member of the Tsar's personal staff, army business I suppose, but he never told us much about his job. I was asked to go with him so that I could be a companion for the afternoon to the Grand Duchess Olga

Nikolayevna. She was the Tsar's eldest daughter and my own age. The royal children didn't go out much; their mother thought St Petersburg society too fast. We spent the afternoon talking and Olga showed me the family apartments . . .'

'They're the ones behind the closed doors, aren't they,' said Emily.

'Are they?' said Mrs Hannay (a little evasively, Emily thought). 'Wherever they are, they were not very interesting after all. Even the secret way out from the Palace to the river that had been built after the earlier Revolution in 1905; it was just a corridor full of old furniture. That was all. My father returned. He looked very happy, I remember, as though he had been given good news.' Then she added quietly, 'Perhaps it was the news of his promotion.'

She started to fold her table napkin.

'They were all killed, weren't they?' Emily said.

'The Royal Family? Yes they were. Father, mother and five children.'

'Couldn't they have escaped through the secret passage?'

'I don't think they wanted to escape. Besides, they were not at the Winter Palace when the Revolution started. They were at Tsarskoe Selo – Tsar's village – where we are going tomorrow. It's called Pushkin now.'

Later, in bed with the curtains open and the winter moonlight filling the room, Alyce said: 'We are so close to the answer but we can't see it. There is something that somebody said today that is a clue. I'm sure of that. But I can't remember what it was.'

'Something Mrs Hannay said?' Emily asked.

'No, I don't think so, unless . . .'

'Unless what?'

'Nothing.'

'Come on Alyce, you can't say that.'

'Well, it's too far fetched really, but you remember her father's second-in-command – Bazorov or something – perhaps he's still alive and she has come for . . .' she hesitated before adding rather unconvincingly, 'well, for revenge.'

Emily snorted. 'That *is* too far-fetched!'

They were silent. Emily, half-sitting up with her pillow propped against the head-board so that she could look out of the window, let her eyes rest on the long, dark shape of the Winter Palace. Somewhere out there was the answer to the riddle: something that happened sixty years ago, some deed still not forgotten, some business that was still unfinished.

Ten

They discovered the solution to the riddle much sooner than either of them had expected.

The Tsar's village was a disappointment. The Summer Palace was still being restored and there was nothing to do there except take photographs of the exterior and tramp through the snow-banked grounds. After ten minutes or so, the tourists returned to the coach and were driven off to Pavlovsk where – Ilsa assured them – the Palace of the Grand Duke Paul had been completely restored.

It was a pleasant change to be out of the city, though the countryside, with its great sweeps of snow-covered land and long, white horizons was like the city in one respect – its scale was superhuman. Between Pushkin and Pavlovsk there were no farms or proper villages (where did the peasants live? Emily wondered) and the woods through which the road passed were darkly monotonous.

The Grand Duke's Palace at Pavlovsk was an immediate success. Even before you went inside you could ride over the snow in a horse-drawn sledge for two rubles, fifty kopecks. Shamus and Jonathan sprang in and were whisked away by two finely built, high stepping horses. Seeing the boys go, Emily thought they looked like Russian princes with their thick fur hats and fair-skinned faces.

The Palace was not on the grand scale of those in

Leningrad. Its modest size, its formal, classical style and delightful setting in wooded parkland gave it the appearance of an English country house of the eighteenth century. It had been battered almost to ruins by the 'Hitler forces' in 1944. Before they retreated, they had placed their explosives in such a way as to do the maximum damage – just for the sake of it. But after the war the Russians had restored the Palace with the same skill and care they had lavished on the rebuilding of Leningrad itself. In each of the restored rooms, there was a large photograph to show how the room had looked after the German withdrawal.

Visitors to the Palace were required to put on rope-soled sandals over their boots to protect the polished wooden floors. The tourists made heavy weather of this simple operation and there was delay while the less supple members fell about the cloakroom as though they had lost their sense of balance. Emily took the opportunity of asking Mr Oblamov a question that she and Alyce had prepared. They had decided that if he was asked straight out whether he had visited the Palace before he would probably be taken by surprise and answer 'No.'

'Many times,' replied Mr Oblamov, turning on Emily the melancholy brown eyes that might have belonged to a poet but not to a policeman. 'Many times, because Intourist officials must make regular visits to the historical sites. The work of restoration is always advancing.'

'But have you always been an Intourist man?' Emily asked, making the best of a bad job.

'No, I have also taught English in the University of Leningrad and I have been in London, at University College in Gower Street. Do you know that?'

'I expect Daddy does,' said Emily, her voice flat with disappointment.

The tour moved off, padding softly through the exquisite rooms. The small scale, the gentle, pastel colours of the decoration, above all the furniture which was dark wood inlaid with lighter patterns and which was set ready for use – the bureau open, the chair pushed back a little from the table – all combined to give the Palace the atmosphere of an elegant home whose owners had stepped out for a walk through the park. The only unexpected feature was the large picture gallery that followed the shallow curve of the south front of the building.

'Oh no! Not more pictures,' cried Shamus.

Ilsa did not need prompting. She led her group through the gallery at a brisk pace. But Emily, still recoiling from the bland assurance with which Mr Oblamov had answered her question, drifted along moodily some way behind. Her eyes ran along the pictures like a stick drawn along the railings: the figures and scenes flicked by without making individual impressions. It was all the more surprising that one face among so many should connect. She stopped dead and stared. Then she glanced forward to see where the others had got to; they were already disappearing round the curve of the gallery. Then she looked back at the painting. Two girls, aged sixteen and seventeen, perhaps, one standing, the other sitting at a table, were in a room that was full of spring sunlight. The sunlight was everywhere, pouring in through the open window, reflecting from the white walls and white tablecloth, sparkling on the glass bowl that held fresh-cut flowers.

It was the face of the seated girl that had caught Emily's attention. She was looking straight at the artist, with her bare forearms resting on the table. Looking back into those eyes, Emily had no doubt. Though the hair was jet black and the young face firm and unlined, the blue eyes, so similar in colour to a fine summer sky at its most distant and pure, were unmistakably those of Mrs Hannay.

Curse the Russian letters! Emily struggled to decipher the inscription but she did not have even the most elementary knowledge of the Russian alphabet. She would have to ask Ilsa to come back and translate but that might draw everyone's attention to the painting, not least Mrs Hannay's and Mr Oblamov's. She looked back the way she had come. The second group from their hotel could not be far behind. Perhaps she could ask their guide to translate.

She waited, listening for the approach of the second group. But it was Ilsa who appeared.

'Are you all right?' Ilsa asked, 'the others are going downstairs now. We have finished the tour of the Palace.'

'What does that say?' Emily asked, pointing to the inscription.

'This is a painting by the Russian master, Valentin Serov,' Ilsa replied patiently. 'Do you like it?'

'But who is it of?'

'The two daughters of Prince Nicolai Dubinsky. They were members of the old nobility before the Great October Socialist . . .'

But Emily had started to run. She could not wait to tell Alyce she had discovered Mrs Hannay's real name and in her excitement she forgot where she had heard the name before.

But Alyce had not. She was already outside, waiting for Emily to join her in the horse-drawn sledge.

'Come on. Mummy's paying,' she called.

'I've got something to tell you,' said Emily, collapsing onto the flat leather cushion beside her sister.

The man cracked his thin whip in the air and the horses started forward. The sledge moved slowly at first but gathered momentum smoothly, the fall of the horses' hooves muffled by the snow. As the sledge moved further and further away from the Palace, the voices of the other tourists faded and the girls were aware of the silence of the snow-filled sunlight.

'Are you sure it was Dubinsky?' Alyce asked calmly when Emily had told her.

'Of course I'm sure. Ilsa translated it.'

'Don't you realise what that means?'

Emily looked blank. The sledge made a wide arc at the end of its run and headed back towards the Palace.

'Dubinsky,' said Alyce with maddening superiority, 'where have you heard that before?'

'Come on Alyce, for heaven's sake. I found out what her name was.'

'The Madonna and Child,' said Alyce, unruffled but excited, 'it belonged to the Dubinsky family.'

'Which one?' Emily was furious with herself for not catching on at once.

'The Leonardo. It was worth a million rubles, don't you remember. The family sold it to Tsar Nicholas for the Museum.'

The million rubles focussed Emily's memory immediately. When she realised the significance of what she had discovered she couldn't refrain from shouting at Alyce that the money had never been paid.

'Don't shout, Emily. We don't want everyone to hear.'

The sledge was nearing the Palace. Shamus and Jonathan were running towards it over the snow.

'So that's why she has come to Russia,' said Emily; 'it's her painting and she's come to take it back.'

Eleven

❧

They arrived back at the Alexander Pushkin Hotel in time for lunch. With a free afternoon in front of them before the official visit to the Kirov Ballet in the evening, the family lingered over their meal. This was not to Emily's liking. She wanted to get on with the business of checking her morning's discovery. After the first excitement, Alyce had – characteristically, Emily thought – begun to doubt whether the face of the girl in the painting had been that of Mrs Hannay. She had insisted that they should check Mrs Hannay's identity before taking any further steps. There was a simple way of checking; they had only to ask at the Reception Desk for Mrs Hannay's passport – a white lie about her telling them to collect it would do – and then look for her maiden name on the first page.

But when the family at last left the table, some to rest, others to read or to write postcards, this simple plan quickly proved unsuccessful. The girl behind the Reception Desk had no intention of handing over anyone's passport; passports would be returned on the day of departure and not before. Emily had the impression that the passports were not there at all.

The girls were obliged to fall back on their second scheme. It was more clumsy and required more preparation, including an expedition to the House of Books on Nevsky Prospekt. Ilsa assured them that they would be able to buy what they needed there and that one of the supervisors would speak English.

The walk from the hotel to the bookshop brought home to them for the first time the full force of the bitter cold. They had been used to being transported here and there in coaches and taxis, seldom spending longer than a few minutes in the open air. But now their strength was soon sapped by the cold so that distances seemed greater than when measured with the eye: the bridge across the Neva took ten minutes to cross and the Palace Square, that had looked no great size a day or two ago, would not surrender easily for all their brisk walking.

Even the Nevsky Prospekt itself seemed to have widened since they drove along it in the coach. It was so wide in fact that they were not sure how to cross. The traffic was light, only a few cars and single-decker trolley buses, but for this reason the cars moved fast. There were no islands on which to shelter half way across, and if pedestrians were allowed to cross from one side of the street to the other, it was not clear to Alyce and Emily how they were supposed to do so.

'We can't just stand here,' said Emily. Her cheeks, that for the first part of the journey had shone ruddy in the freezing air, now felt numb, and beneath the fur lining of the flaps her ears ached with cold.

They chose their moment and ran across. Whistles blew, deep men's voices shouted incomprehensible Russian, shoppers stopped to gape at this extraordinary event.

'Keep going,' Emily growled between her teeth as though the two girls were desperadoes breaking from jail.

A motor-cycle policeman, enormous in his blue-grey greatcoat and shining black boots, was waiting for them on the other side. His words may have been lost on them

but his meaning was quite clear. There was a place for pedestrians to cross – and here he pointed down the street to the mouth of an underpass clearly marked – and it was against the law to cross at any other point. Emily assumed a look of innocence. The policeman glowered at her through his goggles. He was not a teacher to be swayed by a sweet smile and a single dimple. He said something that conveyed a warning, and then kicked off into the thin line of traffic.

'That was a close one,' Emily commented with satisfaction.

The House of Books had three floors. On the third floor the girls found the stationery department and selected from the counter a small white plain card and envelope to match. They asked the assistant if she spoke English. She shook her head but raised her hand to indicate that they should not go away. The supervisor was called. She was very much the woman of authority, dressed all in black and strongly built. She moved behind the counter with the slow stateliness of a great liner coming in to berth.

Emily handed her a piece of paper.

'Could you write this on the card please, in Russian.'

The supervisor scrutinised the message carefully, as though she thought it might be in code.

'Why do you want this?'

'For a friend,' Emily replied. The less said the better was always a good guide.

The supervisor placed the paper on the counter and copied its message on to the card. She wrote slowly, lifting her pen every few letters, though whether this was because she was unfamiliar with the English alphabet or because she still had doubts about the wisdom of what she was doing, Emily could not guess. On the card she wrote in Russian: 'Please meet me in the foyer in the first interval', and then she addressed the envelope to 'Princess Dubinsky'.

The Kirov Ballet was the finest in Russia, finer than the Bolshoi in Moscow (so Ilsa told them). The greatest ballerinas of the past, Pavlova and Ulanova, first danced at the Kirov and it was still the highest ambition of the young dancers of Leningrad to be a member of the famous company. The Leningraders supported their ballet with unswerving loyalty and sought eagerly for news about the stars. The atmosphere outside the theatre and in the foyer was one of intense anticipation; even the struggle to hand in coats and hats, which was just as tough and uncompromising as at the Winter Palace, did not blunt the mood of cheerful excitement with which the crowd entered the calm splendour of the auditorium. The interior was decorated in blue and gold. The rich colouring and extravagant style belonged to the days before the Revolution but if you looked carefully at the crest in front of the Royal Box you saw that the Two-Headed Eagle of the Romanov Tsars had been replaced by a golden Hammer and Sickle.

Emily stood looking up at the tiers of boxes that rose one above the other, forming a series of horse-shoes open to the stage. In the stalls and in the boxes the seats were individual chairs upholstered in peacock blue. The family had a box on the lowest tier to the left of the stage. After some argument about who should sit where, they settled down to enjoy the scene. A minute or two before eight o'clock, Emily excused herself with an incoherent mumble and slipped out of the box to the white-walled corridor that ran behind. Mrs Hannay was two boxes away. The door of that box was closed. Emily took the small envelope from the sleeve of her dress and, bending down, slid the envelope under the door. Then she hurried back to resume her seat.

The lights in the auditorium dimmed, the conductor raised his baton and the members of the orchestra lifted their instruments into position. When the brief overture had been played, the great curtains rose to reveal a vast stage with giant scenery to match. In a Spanish room, cool in shadow, with walls towering into the darkness, Don Quixote was being assisted into his breastplate and helmet by Sancho Panza.

Emily glanced at the occupants of Mrs Hannay's box; their faces, lit by the glow from the footlights, were set unswervingly towards the stage. It was clear to Emily that the envelope had not been noticed and would not be until the start of the interval. She sat back and watched the ballet.

The figure of Don Quixote intrigued her. With his exceptionally long legs, he moved over the stage with giant strides carrying his tall lance and putting his hand to his forehead as though peering into the future where heroic deeds would be achieved. The story moved effortlessly from one joyous scene to another. The music was full of melody, the dancing marvellously agile. The foolish knight rode a real horse through the colourful make-believe.

Emily would have preferred the cinema, but she relaxed and enjoyed the spectacle while her thoughts turned to Mrs Hannay. Typical Emily, the family would say when they heard of her detective work and she would take it, as it was intended, as a compliment. Had she, by sheer good luck – no! By using her wits – discovered something about Mrs Hannay and the picture in the Winter Palace that was not only important but dangerous to know? Of course it was jumping to conclusions to say that Mrs Hannay was going to steal the Dubinsky Madonna from the Palace but at least it was possible that this was her real reason for coming back to Russia after so long. She must have reckoned that even though the Russians were bound to discover her true identity, they would never suspect an old lady of planning the theft of a painting worth a million rubles.

'Two million by now,' Emily muttered.

'Shh!' Siobhan hissed.

Emily glanced at Mrs Hannay's box. Did Mrs Hannay look like a princess?

The clapping broke out simultaneously throughout the theatre. The stars of the first act came out between the curtains to acknowledge the applause. The lights in the auditorium came on. The audience stood and talked and moved towards the exits.

'Are you coming, dears?' asked their mother.

'Where?'

'Just to look around.'

'I think I'll stay here for the interval,' said Alyce.

So it had been arranged: Alyce to watch Mrs Hannay's reaction to the letter, while Emily positioned herself as invisibly as possible in the foyer.

Emily had some difficulty escaping from her mother, but still she was sure she had reached the foyer in good time. It was already crowded and she pushed across to the farthest corner where she could pretend to be studying the photographs of past productions while keeping one eye on the entrance to the boxes.

She waited. The photographs were full of warriors with round shields and spiked helmets. Were the warriors engaged in an opera or a ballet? They did not look capable of either. She looked quickly at the entrance. People were still coming from the boxes but Mrs Hannay was not among them. The warriors wore animal hides and had bare feet. Emily thought that the helmets and bare feet did not go well together. What was the point of wearing a helmet if your enemy could stamp on your toes?

She looked again. Mrs Hannay had paused in the entrance to the foyer. As Emily watched, she raised the white envelope with a slow, deliberate motion. The envelope had been opened: you could see the torn edge. Emily had no doubt that this gesture was intended as a signal and for a moment she forgot she had sent the envelope herself and half expected someone to step forward from the crowd to greet the Princess Dubinsky.

Twelve

❧

'Mr Oblamov is a policeman,' said Alyce in a most solemn and confidential voice.

'And he is watching you,' said Emily.

Mrs Hannay appeared to be neither surprised nor frightened by this information.

She said: 'I think you may be right. They're very touchy about people from the old Russia. He's certainly very keen not to let me out of his sight. It must be a dull job for him.'

'It must be annoying,' Emily murmured, taken aback that their dramatic revelation should meet with such a calm response.

They had decided that the only way to find out whether Mrs Hannay was going to do something about the Leonardo (even between themselves they did not like to use the word 'steal') was to warn her against Mr Oblamov. According to Emily's theory, Mrs Hannay would have no choice but to take the girls into her confidence. Not that they wanted to be involved; even Emily recognised that you didn't play games with the Russian police. To be in the know would be exciting enough.

It had taken them most of the day to catch Mrs Hannay alone. They had found her in mid-afternoon in the Tea Room on the top floor of the hotel. It was a small room dominated by a great silver samovar, from which the waitress dispensed tea in wide, shallow cups. The win-

dows commanded a superb view of the city. It was that time in the afternoon when the setting sun shone brilliantly on the slim spires of the Admiralty and the Cathedral of St Peter and St Paul. As the girls were talking to Mrs Hannay, the sun sank into the grey clouds on the horizon, appearing to disperse them by its fall and bathing the whole western sky in a rich golden light.

'He's only doing his duty,' said Mrs Hannay after a while, the familiar phrase discouraging even further any hope that she might have cause to be anxious about Mr Oblamov's watchfulness.

'But wouldn't it be nice to escape from him, just for once?' Emily asked.

'It would be nice.'

'Perhaps we could help,' said Emily.

Alyce frowned. This was going further than they had agreed.

'Could you?' said Mrs Hannay as though she neither wanted nor expected a reply.

'We only have two more days,' Emily pointed out, ignoring Alyce's scowl.

'Yes.' Mrs Hannay's interest sounded no more than polite. She was either playing a part or had never allowed the possibility of stealing the Leonardo to cross her mind.

Emily stared dejectedly out of the window. The winter sunset might have been a blank wall for all the impression it made on her. What was the point of a holiday without adventure? You might as well have stayed at home. There were friends there and things to do and English food.

'I have an idea.' Mrs Hannay's voice was suddenly alive with enthusiasm. As Emily turned to look at her face, hardly believing, Mrs Hannay went on. 'Let's play a trick on Mr Oblamov. It'll keep him on his toes. He's had it much too easy these few days shadowing an antique like me. He's probably telling his colleagues down at headquarters what a soft assignment it is. Well, we'll show him. Are you two game? You'll get into no trouble, I promise you that, but just for one evening we'll prove that we're cleverer than our friend Mr Oblamov.'

Emily's blue eyes burned with joy. Nothing Mrs Hannay could have said would have suited her better. Without so much as a glance in Alyce's direction, she said:

'What do we have to do?'

'Splendid!' exclaimed Mrs Hannay, and turned to Alyce.

'Yes, all right,' said Alyce cautiously, 'as long as we don't have to do anything wrong.'

'Nothing even faintly wrong or illegal, trust me on that. Just a little encouragement to Mr Oblamov to join in things more. I don't think he's enjoying himself enough, do you? But first, what about some tea? It tastes quite different from a samovar, you know. And I can recommend those small cakes; they're more delicious than they look.'

With instinctive professionalism they talked of other matters while the waitress set two new places at the table. Two cups of tea were brought and a fresh plate of cakes. Emily sank her teeth into the soft, sweet coconut.

'When . . .?' she began as soon as the waitress had withdrawn.

'Tomorrow evening,' Mrs Hannay replied, leaning forward and keeping her voice down, 'when we go to the Circus. The Americans went last night and they have given me an idea. The tourists are always placed in the front row. At one point in the programme – I am not sure when – Popov, the Clown, chooses a 'volunteer' to help him with his act. The Americans say he always tries to pick a tourist; it makes the Leningraders laugh. Now this is the point: Popov always chooses a small man in a dark suit.'

'Why?' Emily asked.

'I gather the volunteer has to look like the dummy that Popov uses for the trick. A harness is lowered from the roof on a long rope and fitted under the volunteer's shoulders. Then a screen is put round him and almost at once he goes shooting upwards at great speed. It isn't him, of course, but the dummy, though the switch is done so quickly the audience don't realise it at first. They think a terrible mistake has been made; the dummy looks so like the volunteer.'

'Who looks so like Mr Oblamov!' cried Emily, her eyes blazing now.

'Exactly,' said Mrs Hannay.

The sun had set. Grey clouds, dark as iron, had re-established themselves on the horizon. The north face of the Winter Palace was dark too. Only on the ice of the river was there a trace of colour, as though the setting sun had left a stain.

Alyce had numerous objections. There was no guarantee that Mr Oblamov would be chosen. He might even be known to Popov, in which case the clown would deliberately choose someone else.

'That is where you come in,' said Mrs Hannay.

'How?'

'You must sit next to Mr Oblamov. No, don't say you can't. It's just a question of being in the right place at the right time. I am sure Emily has a talent for that. He will not suspect anything. If you can sit one on either side of him, so much the better. When Popov comes over to the tourist seats you must make him choose Mr Oblamov.'

'That *is* impossible,' Alyce argued.

'No, it isn't,' Emily challenged her sister, 'we can catch Popov's eye, we can point to Mr Oblamov, we can even push him forward.'

'Oh, come on Emily!'

'Well, you're so feeble, Alyce, you don't want to try anything. It's easy. We can get all the family, and the others, to shout, "We want Mr Oblamov". We don't have to tell them why we're doing it, just that it'll be a good joke, that's all.'

Alyce had no chance to shoot that down because Mrs Hannay cut in at once: 'It'll give me five minutes, perhaps more,' she said. 'I can slip out, collect my coat and be in a taxi before Mr Oblamov knows that I've gone.'

'Where will you go?' Emily asked.

'I shall go and talk to some real Russians. There are Russians in London but they are like me, just ghosts from the past. I want to know what the modern Russians feel; I want to know what it is like to live in the city where I was born. I shall go to the Astoria Restaurant. Ilsa tells me it is still one of the liveliest places in Leningrad. It's just the other side of the river, close to the Winter Palace.'

Conveniently close, Emily thought.

Thirteen

As Emily had anticipated, a furious argument broke out the moment they were alone in their room. Alyce said Emily had gone too far. What would happen to them if Mrs Hannay really was planning to steal the Leonardo? That wouldn't be such a joke. They might be put in prison in Russia for the rest of their lives.

'Don't be ridiculous,' Emily exploded, all the more violently because she was uncertain just what to believe about Mrs Hannay's intentions.

'She knows a secret passage,' Alyce reminded her, 'it's not impossible. And even if she is not going to break into the Winter Palace herself, how do we know that she isn't going to meet the real thief in the Astoria Restaurant? And *we* would have helped them.'

'No, not just us,' Emily corrected her, 'everyone will be shouting for Mr Oblamov.'

'You try telling that to the police,' said Alyce gloomily.

Emily slept badly and woke often. In the dark morning she was inclined to think that Alyce's fears might be well founded. They would have to speak to Mrs Hannay at breakfast and tell her that they could not help her after all. But when she saw Mrs Hannay sitting alone at the round table for eight and Mrs Hannay gave her a brief, pointed glance – nothing so amateur as a wink – her fears calmed and her spirits rose. She said nothing about the evening's plan.

The day passed slowly. The Hall of White Columns in

the Smolny Institute where Lenin had proclaimed the Revolution left Emily unmoved. The interior of St Isaac's Cathedral which Siobhan pronounced 'superb' reminded Emily of the gold painted interior of the flea-pit cinema off Victoria Street. Even the Peter and Paul Fortress with its grim dungeons and small photograph at each cell door to show which revolutionary had been imprisoned there, was of no more than passing interest (though she was amused to see that the sight of the prison cells made Alyce's expression more gloomy than ever). It was the Field of Mars, which they visited in the late afternoon dusk that touched Emily's imagination. In the centre of this enormous square, once the parade ground of the Tsar's regiments, an eternal flame swayed violently this way and that in the icy wind as a memorial to all those who lost their lives in the nine hundred day siege. Six hundred thousand people died, but this – Ilsa reminded them – was only a fraction of the twenty million Russians who perished in the Great Patriotic War against Germany.

Emily gazed at the flame which tugged wildly at its roots as though trying to break free. Twenty million! Everything about Russia was on the grand scale, even the dead. How modest, domestic and friendly the memory of England seemed at that moment.

In one respect the day's tour had been entirely satisfactory. It had proved easy to win support for the idea that Mr Oblamov should be encouraged to volunteer at the circus. No doubt the enthusiasm had been inspired partly by the thought that if Mr Oblamov was chosen no one else would find themselves in that embarrassing position. Even Alyce had been encouraged by the response. By the time they left the hotel for the circus, an extensive plot had been organised so that when Mr Oblamov boarded the coach and sat – as he always sat – in the swivel seat next to the driver, the passengers exchanged knowing looks and suppressed smiles of anticipation.

The Leningrad State Circus, though not as well known as its rival in Moscow, was regarded as one of the best in the world. Its permanent home was a large, domed building on the banks of the Yekaterininski Canal. The coach drew up outside and the passengers charged the entrance like well-drilled troops. A few days in Russia had taught them that a combined attack on the counter was the best method of ensuring a swift victory in the battle to hand in their coats.

The seats rose steeply all round the ring. High above the ring were two platforms with trapezes tied up to them and a number of other ropes hanging loose. Despite their vigorous and well-planned entry, the tourists found that the circus was almost full. It was the school holidays and whole families had come together.

'Look at the Russian children,' Siobhan said, as they stood in the entrance trying to locate their seats.

'What about them?' Emily asked, keeping an eye on Mr Oblamov.

'They're so well behaved,' Siobhan declared, as if a swift glance had told her everything, 'not like children in England.'

'This way please.' Mr Oblamov led the party round the edge of the ring with Emily and Alyce close at his heels. When he reached the row reserved for them, Mr Oblamov stood aside to allow the girls to pass. Emily took his arm as calmly as if he had been her own father.

'Come and sit with us, Mr Oblamov, it's our last night.'

At first it seemed as though he would refuse. He slipped out of Emily's hold and raised both hands, palms forward, as a buffer between his official duties and this presumptuous girl. But he was overwhelmed by a popular demand. All the tourists within range urged him to accept Emily's proposal. He must relax once in a while. He had been such a good host. He had earned an evening without responsibility. The demand was such (not least because the tourists behind Emily wished to gain their seats before the lights went down) that Mr Oblamov surrendered. He raised his hands higher still as if to say that this matter was now outside his control and followed Emily along the row.

He sat between the two girls, with their mother and the rest of the family on Alyce's left. Emily had expected to find herself at the end of the row, but Mrs Hannay had arrived there first by a different route.

'What excellent seats, Mr Oblamov,' said Mrs Hannay as they all sat down.

He looked relieved to find her close at hand.

'It is our policy,' he said with an air of satisfaction.

There was a roll of drums and a series of triumphant chords from the band that was perched on a platform over one of the entrances to the ring. The lights went down and a single spot shone on the opposite entrance. The audience was silent. For a moment or two nothing appeared from the mouth of the tunnel beyond the spotlight. Then, with strange cries and a soft thundering of hooves on the sawdust, the Leningrad State Circus poured into the ring: Cossack horses, grey lumbering elephants that looked unhappy at the pace demanded of them, jugglers and acrobats, dogs that ran round the low wall of the ring, more horses, smaller this time with neat high-stepping movements and jingling bridles, and finally the clowns. When the ring was full, all the humans

and animals turned to face the entrance from which they had emerged. The drums rolled once again. Out of the tunnel walked a large clown with a black top hat and enormous flapping shoes. He was greeted with enthusiastic applause, adults and children clapping their hands as hard as they could bear. The clown took the microphone from the Master of Ceremonies and said three words in a deep, round voice to which the audience responded with a great shout that might have risen from the throats of warriors welcoming their chief.

This surely was the famous Popov.

The ring emptied and the show began. Emily glanced at the programme but there was no way she could spot Popov's appearance and she did not wish to ask Mr Oblamov or Mrs Hannay to translate. Item after item passed, but Popov did not reappear. Emily calculated that the interval must be approaching and she feared that Mr

Oblamov might take that opportunity to change seats. The Cossack horsemen were riding round and round the ring at astonishing speed, leaping on and off their horses, riding back to front, even standing on the saddle with one hand holding the rein while the other waved wildly above the head. Emily tried to catch Mrs Hannay's eye but the fine aristocratic features were looking straight ahead, keen with pleasure and appreciation of the performance.

The horsemen finished their act and rode off at such high speed it seemed they could not help colliding with the outside wall of the building. It was now or never, Emily decided, fixing her eyes on the dark tunnel and willing Popov to appear. But two other clowns came out of the darkness, one carrying a live chicken by the legs, the other with what looked like a small seesaw under his arm. They were followed – to Emily's relief – by Popov, who sauntered into the ring, acknowledging the welcome by raising his top hat to reveal a second chicken on the top of his head. The bird flapped its wings once before Popov covered it again with his hat.

For a few minutes the two lesser clowns entertained the audience, their efficient but commonplace antics whetting the appetite for the genius who was to follow. There was no sign of the screen Emily had expected, but high above the ring the harness was hanging loose a little below the level of the trapezes.

In due course the lesser clowns were dismissed. They hurried away leaving the chicken and the seesaw behind them in the centre of the ring. As Popov approached, the chicken stepped on to one end of the seesaw and, almost at once, was propelled into the air by a sharp downward pressure on the other end by Popov's enormous shoe. Popov lifted his hat. The resident chicken flew to the ground, making way for its partner, which landed on the clown's head with such accurate ease it might have been doing this extraordinary manoeuvre since birth. Popov replaced his hat and looked about him as though nothing unusual had occurred.

This trick was repeated three times to the delight of the audience before Popov released the chickens from their routine. Two attendants raced into the ring, like ball-boys at a tennis championship, sweeping up the chickens and the seesaw without a check in their running and disappearing into the tunnel under the band's platform.

Popov took the microphone again and made an announcement that caused a stir of excitement. Emily was sure that the moment had come. Popov crossed the ring towards the tourists' seats, while behind him the two attendants reappeared with a four-sided canvas screen which they placed with obvious care on an exact spot.

Popov spoke in English. 'Now I am asking the visitors to our city if one of them will help me. Is there a brave man among you who does not fear the heights?'

Shamus was out of his seat and into the ring before anyone could prevent him. His action, swift and unexpected, stopped all the mouths that were about to call on Mr Oblamov to volunteer. Emily cursed inwardly. She had not told the twins about the plan because she did not trust them to keep the secret. Now there was nothing she could do but watch; and as it was her nature to swing violently from excitement to despair, she at once abandoned any hope that the situation could be corrected.

Popov welcomed Shamus with a formal handshake. He said something in Russian which prompted a round of applause. Then he spoke in English. 'I congratulate this brave young man but for this experiment it is necessary to have a grown man. What about you sir?'

He pointed straight at Mr Oblamov, just as if he had himself been a member of the plot. Emily raised her hand in response, crying out, 'Yes – Mr Oblamov!'

Once again Mr Oblamov found himself the object of popular acclaim and once again he found it impossible to refuse. When he made as if to decline, voices on all sides called on him to accept the challenge. There would have been no need for Alyce and Emily to say anything, so loud and persistent was the chorus of 'Mr Oblamov! Mr Oblamov!'

With a neat smile of resignation, Mr Oblamov stepped forward and into the ring, followed by the cheers not only of the tourists but of the whole arena. He cast one glance over his shoulder at Mrs Hannay and then squared himself to face the ordeal. Emily noticed that he did not say a word to Popov, perhaps because he was waiting until they were within the privacy of the screen.

The harness was lowered from the roof and fitted under Mr Oblamov's arms. The screen was placed around him and almost immediately – too quickly, Emily was sure, for the harness to have been transferred – a body was drawn upwards at speed. For a moment she was certain some dreadful mistake had been made and that it was indeed Mr Oblamov's small, dark-suited figure that was now level with the trapezes and still rising. Then the body disappeared into the shadows of the roof and the audience looked down again at the ring, their minds still wavering. The screen was opened and Mr Oblamov stepped out into the spotlight unharmed. He was looking across the ring to his seat but the spotlight was dazzling and he was trying to shield his eyes against the glare.

Only then did Emily notice that Mrs Hannay had gone.

Fourteen

It was agreed that Mr Oblamov had been a good sport. Emily knew that he had gone straight out at the interval to telephone from the ticket office – she had kept an eye on him while allowing herself to be pulled along by the tide of Russians who used the interval to walk up and down in the foyer – but he had returned to the same seat and had made no reference to Mrs Hannay's departure. Back at the hotel the tourists had invited him to join them for a drink.

This mood of cheerful comradeship renewed itself in the morning. As is often the case on an overseas tour, the day of departure for home was the signal for people to discover unexpected virtues in their fellow travellers. Addresses were exchanged. An air of joviality characterised the members of the party whenever they met in the corridors and public rooms. Though they told one another that they were sorry to be leaving, there was still a whole day to enjoy as their flight did not depart until the evening.

Emily and Alyce reported to Mrs Hannay on how Mr Oblamov had reacted to her disappearance and she told them about her visit to the Astoria Restaurant. She did not seem concerned about the telephone call he had made – 'Just warning headquarters that I was on the loose', she commented – and she had much enjoyed being free of her shadow for a while. She had met a group of Russians from Kiev. They had dined with her and, after dinner, she had shown them the Winter Palace and the Admiralty.

The plan – Emily thought – had worked perfectly. Mr Oblamov appeared to have no hard feelings. On the contrary he moved from table to table at breakfast in obvious good humour. He was something of a hero, a role he appeared to enjoy. When he came to the family's table he said 'Good morning' with such bright sincerity it was impossible to doubt his goodwill. He hoped that their final day in Leningrad would be an interesting one.

'Will you come with us to the airport?' Emily thought to ask.

'Oh yes, I must see you safely on the 'plane.'

If he knew that the Dubinsky Madonna had been stolen, he was playing a very cool game. Emily caught Mrs Hannay's eye and her heart jumped. The anxiety on Mrs Hannay's normally so controlled features was unmistakable.

Mr Oblamov moved to the next table. Cheerful cries greeted him.

'This is not goodbye, Mr Oblamov?'

'Oh no, I must see you safely . . .'

Emily excused herself and waited for Alyce in the lounge.

'I'm going back to the Winter Palace,' she announced when Alyce joined her.

'There isn't time,' Alyce argued, 'it's shopping this morning and packing this afternoon; Mummy has just said so.'

'The coach doesn't leave for the airport until six.'

'But what's the point?' Alyce asked.

'To see if the Leonardo's still there.'

Emily spoke lightly, telling the truth but anxious to avoid provoking her sister. Her tactics failed.

'Of course it's still there!' Alyce exploded. She spoke with such force that several guests in the lounge turned to look at the girls and – what was worse – remained attentive to hear Emily's response.

'It'll give us something to do, then,' Emily kept her voice steady and low, 'packing won't take all afternoon.'

It wasn't much of an argument but in the end it proved sufficient. Their mother, misinterpreting their motives, urged them to go as soon as their packing was done. Siobhan had already decided to spend her 'last hours in Russia' visiting an exhibition of Soviet Technology, an alternative that Emily dismissed as 'dead boring'. Penelope preferred to stay and help their mother with the packing and the twins.

It was already half past three when Alyce and Emily crossed the Troitsky Bridge. (Packing had taken longer than Emily had anticipated because Alyce had insisted that they took their cases down to the room on the first floor that was being used as a base for the departing tour.) The setting sun was shining directly into their faces, taking the edge off the bitter cold. The queue to enter the Winter Palace was short – it being less than an hour before closing time – and the girls had no difficulty sailing by the soldier who controlled the door. So far, so good, thought Emily, but then she saw that the attendant on duty at the cloakroom was the same yellow-eyed old dog she had treated with such disrespect on the previous visit. She turned her back on him, took off her coat and handed it to Alyce. 'There's no point both of us going,' she explained.

At the top of the white marble staircase they passed

through the great mahogany doors and into the state rooms. If they kept turning to the left they would come to the room overlooking the river where they had first seen the Leonardo. But after they had passed through a string of rooms, they found themselves in a corridor with windows looking out on a small courtyard.

'This is not the way to the Leonardo,' said Alyce.

Emily stopped, uncertain. In that moment's hesitation the Leonardo was forgotten. She had seen a door in the wall opposite the window and beside it a plain wooden chair, empty. The woman on duty in the corridor had deserted her post. There was no indication that this door would lead to those apartments that, Emily believed, had remained unchanged since the Revolution, but it was worth a try. She walked quickly to the door. The curved

gold handle sank easily under her pressure. As the door opened away from her she stepped through the opening leaving the door ajar for Alyce to follow.

'Come back at once,' said Alyce, making what was clearly a supreme effort to exert her seniority.

'Who says?'

'I do.' Alyce was standing at the opening but with both feet firmly on the corridor side. 'Come out, Emily. You'll get into trouble.'

'At least close the door,' said Emily from within, as though she would refuse to discuss the matter until Alyce had entered the forbidden territory.

A small group of two or three visitors appeared at the far end of the corridor. Emily began to push the door so that Alyce had either to enter the forbidden area or resist the pressure, thus causing a scene. Emily guessed rightly that Alyce would wish to avoid a scene at all costs.

They found themselves at the foot of a flight of stone steps that led upwards towards a landing on which there must have been a window for it was from there that the grey daylight appeared to be coming.

Emily looked at Alyce.

'We can say we're English and that we came in by mistake,' she suggested. She was confident that the tourists would be forgiven all.

Alyce said nothing but her scowl and stiff bearing expressed her attitude clearly enough.

'We can explore,' Emily hurried on, put out by her sister's silence, 'we might even find that secret passage.'

Alyce looked at her watch. 'There are precisely forty minutes before the Palace closes.'

'That still gives us time.'

Alyce's theatrical sigh registered a final protest and

excused herself from blame if anything went wrong.

They climbed the stone steps. From the window on the next landing they could see that the daylight had almost gone and that the light they had seen was coming from other rooms whose windows looked out on to the narrow well. At the top of the next flight there was a white door with a curved handle identical to the one Emily had pressed downstairs. She opened the door cautiously and looked inside. The room, half in shadow, had a low ceiling, plain white walls and a bare wooden floor; in the wall opposite the door were three round windows through which Emily could see the street lamps on the far side of the Palace Square.

'There's nothing there,' said Alyce, looking over Emily's shoulder.

Emily went in all the same. At first it seemed that Alyce was right. When they entered the room, stepping carefully on the bare boards for fear of being heard below, they soon saw that the room was a dead end, with no doors to lead on to further discoveries. There was a fireplace with an enamel surround and a stove standing out in front of the chimney. To the left of the fireplace was a cupboard built into the wall with two narrow doors. That was all. The room had probably belonged to one of the Palace servants in the old days.

Alyce stooped to look out of one of the round windows at the Palace Square below. Emily pulled at one of the cupboard doors, just checking. In such casual actions are the seeds of adventure.

It was not a cupboard but the bottom of a rectangular shaft containing a wooden ladder, fixed vertically, reaching up into the darkness.

The rungs were black with dust.

'You're mad,' said Alyce.

'I know,' said Emily, climbing slowly.

But Alyce followed. After about ten rungs they were in total darkness so that Emily had to feel upwards with her free hand before each step. Three rungs later her hand touched a flat wood surface; she felt more widely and discovered the rectangle of a trap door. She climbed one more rung to give herself some leverage and then pushed upwards with the palm of her hand. The trap rose, but no more than an inch. The weight told her that she would have to climb higher and try to use her shoulders.

'What is it?' Alyce asked from below.

'I'm not sure. An attic, or it may be the roof.'

'You'll freeze if it is,' was Alyce's immediate thought.

Emily used the top of her head and then, as the trap door rose, managed to take the weight on her shoulders. Dark clouds of approaching night and icy air greeted her as she raised the door into a vertical position. She had found her way on to the roof of the Winter Palace.

Fifteen

❧

The roof of the Winter Palace might have been designed by Bartolomeo Rastrelli with adventurous children in mind. The pitch of the roof was not steep and it was easy to walk along without slipping; even if you did slide down there was no danger of falling off, for all round the edge was a stone balustrade. At regular intervals on this balustrade Rastrelli had placed bronze figures and urns whose black shapes stood out against the sombre sky.

'It's fantastic!' Emily exclaimed, standing up straight and catching her first sight of the full length of the roof. All around were the roofs of Leningrad, uniform in height as all palaces had been obliged to follow the Tsar's master plan for the city. There was little chance of her being spotted from these other buildings or from below. The only hazard was the cold.

'We can't be long,' Alyce warned again. She sounded resigned, as though having allowed Emily to come this far, no escapade, however crazy, could make matters worse.

Emily acknowledged the warning with a nod as she set off along the roof. The Palace Square was on her right, the River Neva on her left. The lead surface was slippery in patches but did not look treacherous. It did not worry her that Alyce declined to follow but remained up to her waist in the shaft watching her sister's progress.

Emily did not intend to go far. She had neither coat nor hat and knew at once that the cold would prevent her walking more than a few yards.

She had taken about six steps when she thought she heard Alyce say something, but the phrase, caught by the wind, did not reach her intact and she walked on. The excitement of walking high above the city was like the dreams she sometimes had in which she was flying over the house at home, swooping down like a swallow to the amazement and admiration of the family.

Her right foot stepped on to a thin streak of ice. The foot slipped suddenly away from her and she fell heavily on to the lead. For a second she thought that was the worst of the accident but the slope of the roof that had been so easy to walk across now acted as a slide that drew her body downwards towards the balustrade. Her instinct was to press her hands and feet against the surface to slow her descent, but whether because she had been dazed by the fall or because her will had been numbed by the cold, she failed to do this. Her body gathered momentum. She was on her back, with her head up looking at her feet. Quite calmly she visualised what would happen if the balustrade did not stop her fall: she would spread her arms like wings and fly down to the Palace Square lowering her feet just in time to land on the cobbles.

Her boots hit the stone hard at the base of a bronze statue. She lay still. The immediate danger was past but when she attempted to scramble to her feet, she found that her whole body was shuddering. She tried to control her limbs but could not. Yet every moment she remained in the open the shuddering would get worse.

She managed to turn her head to look for Alyce.

'Are you all right?' the voice from the safety of the shaft seemed to ask.

'I'm OK,' Emily managed to call, though it was as much to convince herself as to assure her sister.

Still shuddering, she worked her way along the flat gutter inside the balustrade, passing bronze figures and urns, until she was level with the trap door. Then she started to climb slowly upwards on all fours. Nearing the top, she called out to Alyce to give her a hand. Alyce stretched out as far as she could to pull Emily up to the opening. In two minutes they were down the shaft and in the servant's room below. They had not bothered to close the trap door.

'Are you all right?' Alyce asked once again.

'I can't stop shivering.'

'We must go down: it's almost closing time.'

Alyce started towards the door but although Emily intended to follow she could not walk. Her head ached and the shuddering seemed to have drained her limbs of strength. Alyce caught her as she was falling.

'I'll be all right in a minute,' Emily murmured as she sank to the floor and sat with one shoulder against the wall. Alyce was not so much unsympathetic as acutely anxious that they should not delay. She proposed to leave Emily and go for help; better to face an angry Russian official, she argued, than be locked in the Winter Palace and risk missing the flight home. But Emily would not have it. Weak though she was, she asserted her will. She told Alyce to help her up and together they shuffled towards the door. The stone steps were more difficult but the girls managed to reach the floor below without stumbling.

Slowly – oh, so slowly – the blood flowed back into Emily's frozen limbs. She knew that the further she descended into the Palace, the warmer it would become, and this gave her the strength to stop the shuddering, at least for a few seconds at a time. Then it would break loose again like an animal she could not control.

They reached the door that would lead them to the corridor. Alyce opened it without hesitation. Too late now to worry whether there was anyone watching.

The corridor was in darkness. It appeared that this part of the Palace had already been closed for the night. But it was warm here and Emily felt better. The shuddering continued but now it was only in shallow ripples that she was able to bring under control without difficulty.

Emily said: 'Someone will still be around. Let's run.'

At first it was like running with pins and needles in both legs but the footfalls seemed to draw life down into the toes. Soon Emily was her old self, though still a little shaken by what had happened.

Their running brought them to the Throne Room which was the first state room they had entered at the top of the white marble staircase. But even in the dim light they could see that the great mahogany doors were closed. Emily grasped the enormous round handle and shook the doors. They were not only locked but bolted to the floor, for all her pulling and pushing could hardly move them.

'There's another way out,' Emily remembered, 'when we came with Ilsa we didn't go down the main staircase.'

There were three exits from the Throne Room: the one behind the throne through which they had just come, the mahogany doors that were firmly closed and an opening – now on their right – that led to the display of armour. The latter they had passed through on their previous visit and though they could not recall where it led, it was the only route that offered any hope.

They were walking now with quick short steps and keeping close together. The great horses with their heavily armoured riders towered above them. In the uneven darkness, the faces of the horsemen seemed watchful and menacing so that the girls were glad to escape to the next gallery where they were forced to turn sharp left and follow a line of smaller rooms overlooking the river.

Emily said: 'This is the right way, I'm sure.'

They hurried from room to room, only half believing now that speed mattered. A black object loomed in front of them.

'What on earth's that?' Alyce exclaimed.

'God knows,' Emily replied, veering to the right to avoid the object. This was no time to bother with the identity of every obstacle. And then she remembered. It was the stand that held the Leonardo painting.

'Wait a minute, Alyce.'

They both turned to look at the glass front of the stand.

The only faces they could see were the reflections of their own. The Leonardo had gone.

Sixteen

If they had discovered earlier in the afternoon that the Dubinsky Madonna was not on its stand, they would probably have argued that there was some perfectly reasonable explanation for the painting's disappearance. But now such a calm response was impossible. The painting had been stolen. Fear of being involved was made a hundred times worse by the fact that they were trapped in the very place from which the painting had disappeared. They leaped to what seemed the obvious conclusion. Mrs Hannay had returned to Russia to reclaim the priceless Leonardo that belonged to her family and she had tricked the girls into helping her.

Their one thought was to escape from the Winter Palace and be reunited with their mother. There was a good chance that their part in the affair would never be known to the police. The sooner they left Russia the better. What would happen to Mrs Hannay they did not know or care.

But first they had to find a way out.

'There's bound to be a night watchman or someone like that,' Emily argued.

'What shall we tell him?' Alyce asked.

'Nothing. We just look lost.' Emily had far more experience of clashing with authorities and she had little faith in explanations, whether false or true. It was safer to act as though explanations were not required.

There was no time for further delay. The coach to the

airport left in under an hour. They ran on in the direction they had been going, passing from room to room, each one an exact copy of the last, like a single room seen in reflecting mirrors. This passage of rooms, reminiscent of a dream in which for all your running no progress is made, caused even Emily to be afraid.

'This place gives me the spooks,' she said aggressively. She was glad to see the head of the staircase at last, though the eeriness of the surroundings was not lessened by the white marble which reminded her of the great white blocks and statues in the Cemetery of St Ignatius behind her school. At the bottom of the staircase there was a wide corridor, at the far end of which a light was visible. They approached the light without caution, talking

loudly. They found themselves back in the entrance hall. The light came from the single naked bulb hanging above the cloakroom. The yellow-eyed old dog of a man was waiting for them to collect their coats. As far as they could tell he was the only other person in the building.

Emily was sure he would remember her, but his yellow eyes might have been blind for all the signals they gave. The coats lay across the counter like two dead birds, their collars hanging over the side, and the attendant had placed one palm flat on each.

'Our coats,' said Emily and grasped the collar of hers in one hand.

But the old man shook his head sharply and pressed down so that Emily could not have pulled the coat free without a struggle.

Alyce lifted her wrist and tapped the face of her watch. The attendant was unimpressed.

Emily said: 'We'll have to snatch them and make a run for it. Which way is the exit?'

'The doors on the right,' Alyce replied, without looking at them.

There was, of course, no guarantee that the doors were unlocked but that was a risk they would have to take.

'I'll give the word,' said Emily, smiling straight into the yellow eyes as though she was talking to the man.

They both lunged forward at the word 'Now!' The old man fought hard but did not have the strength to hold down both coats at once. He kept repeating one word which they took to be a curse, but neither his scraggy hands nor his curses could prevent the girls dragging their coats off the counter.

The exit doors were locked on the inside, but Emily was able to turn the large iron key with a single movement of her wrist. The doors opened away from them and they burst out on to the embankment to the astonishment of a small group of men who were approaching.

The most direct route back to the hotel was to the right along the enbankment and then across the Troitsky Bridge, but this was the direction from which the group of men was approaching. If the attendant called to them to help they would easily block the girls' escape.

'This way, Al,' Emily shouted and turned left towards the Admiralty. She thought that they would be able to work their way round the Palace and reach the Troitsky Bridge by another route.

To their dismay, the attendant did not give up. They heard him shouting. At the west end of the Palace, they turned sharply left towards Palace Square. Behind them was the sound of shouting still, but three or four voices now, including one calling quite clearly in English, 'Halt!'

'I can't run much more,' Alyce gasped when they had covered barely fifty yards of the Palace Square.

'You must,' Emily insisted.

She had seen that there was an exit from the Square much closer than the grand archway that would lead them to Nevsky Prospekt. This other exit seemed to point to the right direction and with luck would have smaller roads or alleyways leading off.

They ran on, keeping close to the south face of the Palace. Alyce was struggling for breath in the frozen air. At last, when they had almost reached the exit road she stopped and stood gasping. Emily stopped a little way ahead and looked behind. The small group of pursuers had stopped, too, near the central entrance to the Palace. But they were not out of breath. They had gathered round a policeman whose burly, blue-grey figure and motor-cycle were visible in the centre of the group.

Even Alyce was prepared to start running again. In the brief pause, the girls had put on their overcoats though there had been no time to button them or pull their fur hats from the pockets.

The exit from the Square brought them to a narrow road flanked by imposing buildings that could once have been the palaces of the nobility or the ministries of the Tsar's government. There were no turnings off that looked sufficiently obscure to provide escape routes. Nor could the girls see where this road was leading, for it curved away to the right some fifty yards ahead.

This uncertainty about where they were going and the prospect of trying to out-run the policeman on his motor-cycle was too much for them both. They stopped again, their hearts thumping against the inside of their chests. The policeman was riding towards them, not bothering to hurry, the engine chugging quietly. He drew up beside them and without dismounting held out a gloved hand.

Emily clutched at a wild hope. 'I think he wants money,' she muttered, as though she knew the ways of the world better than her sister.

'I've only got a few kopecks,' Alyce whispered.

Emily thrust both hands into the pockets of her coat. There was nothing there. She tried the pockets of her woollen trousers. The fingers of her left hand found the metal disc Alyce had been given by the cloakroom attendant. She drew it out and offered it to the policeman.

He nodded. 'Da, da.'

Alyce gave him her disc. He closed his gloved fingers and put the two discs in the pocket of his greatcoat.

Emily looked at Alyce but had the sense not to laugh until the policeman was out of earshot.

'Emily!' Alyce got her word in first for once. 'You ran for nothing.'

But Emily was too seized with laughter to argue. They chuckled happily together as they hurried on along the curving road until they reached the Suvorov Monument and there turned left towards the Troitsky Bridge. They were so pleased with themselves they forgot for a while that they might still be involved in a much more serious matter than failing to hand in their discs at the cloak-room. On the Bridge they joined the jostling flow of Leningraders leaving the city for the northern suburbs. From the far side of the Bridge to the Alexander Pushkin Hotel was only five minutes' walk. They had cut things fine but they approached the hotel in a mood of triumph.

The porter opened one glass door to let them in. The first thing Emily felt was the warmth. The first thing she heard was her mother's voice.

'It's all right, Siobhan,' the voice called, 'they're here. Where on earth have you been, you two? The coach is going in ten minutes. And look at your face, Emily, it's covered with dirt.'

It was not the welcome a brave adventuress had the right to expect.

She said: 'We didn't realise the time.'

Alyce backed her up with an unexpectedly profes-sional lie: they had crossed the wrong bridge and had found themselves in a district that was completely unfamiliar. Emily, avoiding her mother's eye, saw the other members of the tour standing together, watching and talking. They had their hand luggage and their over-coats. They were ready to depart. Mrs Hannay was standing with Penelope and the twins. Seeing her, Emily recalled with a strange mixture of fear and excitement the empty stand from which the Leonardo had disappeared. She looked round at once for Mr Oblamov but could not see him.

'We've brought your shoulder bags down from your room,' their mother was saying, 'but yours hasn't got your passport in, Emily.'

'No, it's in my case.'

'Well, it's no good there,' said her mother sharply.

It seemed to Emily that her mother's anger at their late arrival was being diverted on to the whereabouts of her passport. Glad to encourage this shift, she offered to fetch the passport at once. But her mother would have none of it.

'You go and give your face a good wash with hot water and soap,' she ordered.

'Can I help?' Mrs Hannay asked as she approached. 'I have to put something in my case.'

'No, it's all right. I'll go,' said Emily hastily.

'You certainly will not!' exclaimed her mother. 'You've caused enough trouble already. Give your keys to Mrs Hannay, and go and wash.'

Emily shrugged and slunk away towards the wash-room reflecting on the injustice that made parents' wrath fall upon the first child to hand. Alyce had received hardly so much as an angry glance.

When Alyce entered the wash-room and the door swung to behind her, Emily said, 'Mummy's in a mood.'

'Well, it was rather silly to leave your passport in your case.'

That was typical Alyce. She always sided with authority. But Emily, looking with distaste at the small, flat tablet of Russian soap, decided to curb her tongue. She had something more important to say.

'Mrs Hannay hasn't been arrested,' she said, catching Alyce's eye in the mirror above the basin.

Seventeen

On the coach to the airport Emily pretended to sleep. She *was* tired but she would not risk losing consciousness until the aeroplane had taken off and was heading for England.

Under the guise of sleep she assembled her thoughts. Her teachers called her a lazy thinker and so she was when the subject did not interest her, but when she chose she could use her mind with a method and tenacity that would have left her teachers astonished.

She snuggled low on her seat. She was warm: warm in body and warm in spirit with the satisfaction of a daring adventure successfully completed. There was nothing to fear from the escapade on the roof but it would be better not to boast about it either. It would have to be kept as a secret treasure to be taken out from time to time when life was low. Then the thought of the roof of the Winter Palace and of the bitter cold of the Russian night, and the knowledge that she had been brave enough to face them both, would carry her through the lowest day.

But the Leonardo was another matter. The thought of it made her open her eyes as though she had felt an unexpected pain. They were still in the suburbs of Leningrad.

'Are you awake, Emily?' Alyce asked in a whisper.

'No.'

Emily closed her eyes again. She guessed that Alyce,

too, was anxious about the missing painting – the Mother and Child, the Dubinsky Madonna, the Leonardo. But Mrs Hannay had not been arrested. Was that a good sign? If she had stolen the painting she would not be allowed to leave the country. The Russian authorities knew who she was. Even if they had no evidence against her, putting two and two together would be enough. Perhaps the police were biding their time and would arrest her at the airport.

But had she stolen the painting? Had the painting been stolen at all? In the thick warmth of the coach, surrounded by English people exchanging stories and impressions of their visit to Russia, it was tempting to believe that nothing so dramatic and unusual could possibly have happened. Yet the facts were not easy to ignore: the painting had belonged to the Dubinsky family, still did belong if you accepted the argument about payment, and Mrs Hannay was a member of that family: and the fact that she had – as only the girls knew – cunningly arranged to escape Mr Oblamov on the very night that the Leonardo had disappeared, made the unbelievable only too easy to believe.

Emily tried to visualise the customs hall at the airport. Would they check the luggage of passengers leaving the country? Even if they did, Mrs Hannay would not be caught that way; she would never try to take the Leonardo out of Russia in her own suitcase. She must have been working with someone, perhaps one of the Russians from Kiev she met in the Astoria Restaurant. She had called them tourists, but of course one of them must have been her accomplice. Now everything fell into place once you knew the key. It was this man from Kiev who had done the robbery using the secret passage that only Mrs Hannay knew. When the fuss had died down and long after Mrs Hannay had gone back to England, he would smuggle the painting out of the country. It was small enough to be carried under an overcoat or between the pages of a newspaper.

She sat up so abruptly her mother asked what was the matter.

'Nothing, Mummy, I was just thinking.'

'That'll be the day,' said Siobhan.

'Not something you've left behind, I hope.'

'No, Mummy, just something.'

Emily turned to see where Mrs Hannay was sitting and, as on the journey from the airport a week ago, she found herself looking straight into Mrs Hannay's pale blue eyes. Mrs Hannay didn't smile exactly but with the slightest movement of her features seemed to be saying something. 'Don't worry,' Emily felt sure the movement meant, 'the painting is quite safe.'

Penelope said: 'I thought Mr Oblamov was coming with us to the airport.'

'I know,' said Shamus, 'he's gone to the circus again.'

'It was a wonderful circus, wasn't it?' said their mother.

But Mr Oblamov had not gone to the circus. He was waiting for them in the main hall of the airport, standing near the statue of Lenin. The tourists greeted him with enthusiasm. They had feared that they would not have a chance to thank him and say goodbye. When he led the way to the customs hall, they crowded behind him as though glad to be seen in his company.

In the hall their cases – which had come ahead of them on a separate coach – were arranged in a long row on the floor.

Mr Oblamov raised his voice.

'Please unlock your cases. I regret it is necessary to check all baggage of passengers leaving the Soviet Union.'

There was a rumble of protest but the atmosphere of goodwill that Mr Oblamov and Ilsa had engendered was sufficient to carry the party through this annoying procedure without displays of bad temper.

Emily noticed that Mr Oblamov took his place alongside the uniformed soldiers who were acting as customs officials. She pushed in between Shamus and Jonathan, who shared one case, and put her own case on the table. A soldier clicked open the catches and started to lift the lid but Mr Oblamov said something to him in Russian. The soldier closed the lid and pressed the catches.

'For children, it is not necessary,' said Mr Oblamov, including the twins' case as well as Emily's in his decision. 'Lock your cases, please. They will now go to the aeroplane.'

Much relieved that the shambles in her case had not been exposed to public view or, worse still, to her mother's, Emily watched the soldier put her case on the slow-moving conveyor belt. The next time she saw it would be at Gatwick Airport in England.

'That's unfair!' Alyce exclaimed. She was further along the table and the contents of her own case, so neatly packed, were being searched thoroughly by a young soldier.

Laughing quietly to herself, Emily made way for Mrs Hannay, who had been standing close behind her. Mrs Hannay placed her case on the table and opened the lid herself. Emily did not move away. Of course Mrs Hannay did not have the painting with her but Emily felt compelled to stay and make sure. Mr Oblamov evidently shared Emily's interest. He stood beside the soldier who probed carefully every layer of the case. He completed his search and lowered the lid. Mr Oblamov said to Mrs Hannay: 'I must ask you to go with this officer.'

'For what purpose?' Mrs Hannay asked.

'I regret, in a few cases a personal search is required.'

'And if I do not choose to be searched?' said Mrs Hannay politely.

Mr Oblamov spoke to her in Russian.

'In English please, Mr Oblamov. I am a citizen of the United Kingdom.'

Mr Oblamov looked so sad Emily thought he might burst into tears. Looking down at the table he murmured, 'I am from the State Security Police.'

'You do surprise me, Mr Oblamov,' said Mrs Hannay.

The silence in the customs hall told Mrs Hannay that the other passengers were listening. She gave Mr Oblamov a charming smile which seemed to strike him like a blow for he stepped back and stumbled against the conveyor belt.

'Careful, Mr Oblamov,' Shamus cried out, but Mr Oblamov had no difficulty in steadying himself. Mrs Hannay turned away and followed the officer to a door at the far end of the hall.

'Why does Mrs Hannay have to be searched?' Shamus asked his mother.

'I don't know, dear. Perhaps because she was born in Russia.'

They waited for Mrs Hannay in the departure lounge. The room was thinly furnished with a handful of white plastic chairs and two white circular tables on which were spread pamphlets in various languages describing the life of Vladimir Ilyich Lenin. Shamus and Jonathan seized a number of these pamphlets for their own possession. For the other tourists, the cheerful friendliness that had characterised their relationships since the early morning now gave way to a more reserved manner. Families looked in on themselves. They would soon be returning to their normal lives. They had said goodbye to Ilsa (though few had spoken to Mr Oblamov once it had been revealed that he was a policeman) and they were now in no man's land. Officially they had left Russia for they had handed in their currency forms and cleared their baggage. They would not have been allowed to go back even if Mrs Hannay had called for help.

Emily stood apart. She had placed herself where she could see back into the customs hall and watch the door through which Mrs Hannay had gone. But standing there, watching, was only a gesture. Emily's one thought – and who can blame her? – was to escape from Russia. Though for the sake of the adventure she had convinced herself that Mr Oblamov was a policeman, it had come as a shock to discover that he really was.

The departure of their flight to Gatwick was announced. The tourists pressed forward to obtain the best seats on the aeroplane.

Emily did not move.

'Come on, dear,' her mother said, 'Mrs Hannay can look after herself, I'm sure.'

But Emily lingered as long as she dared, making the point to herself rather than to anyone else. She was the last to leave the departure lounge and climb the steps into the 'plane. At the top of the steps she looked back. She would keep a seat for Mrs Hannay.

The return flight was by a British airline and Emily noted with relief the friendly faces of the crew and the faded but cosy interior of the cabin. She was now on British territory. She sat down and fastened her seat belt at once as though this in some way bound her more securely to her own country.

At last, when it seemed to Emily that the pilot could not possibly delay any longer, Mrs Hannay appeared. The steward closed the cabin door behind her.

'What was all that about?' someone asked.

'Just routine,' Mrs Hannay replied quietly as she walked down the centre of the cabin looking for a seat.

'Here, Mrs Hannay,' Emily called out.

'We thought they had put you in prison,' said Shamus.

The people who heard him laughed at the idea. Emily laughed too. She could afford to laugh now that the aeroplane had begun to move slowly away from the airport building towards the runway.

Eighteen

The flight time from Leningrad to Gatwick was three and a quarter hours. Emily slept much of the way. With Mrs Hannay safe beside her and no danger that the British crew would turn back once they were out of Russian air space and over the Baltic Sea, she surrendered to the exhaustion that was bound to follow so long and exciting a day.

She was too tired now to weigh up the chances of Mrs Hannay having got away with a robbery that in its way was as stupendous as stealing the Crown Jewels; much too tired to think out whether it was robbery at all to take back something that had once belonged to your family. So she let her thoughts drift among the memories of the day; they ran this way and that highlighting fragments of scenes, catching momentarily Russian faces, until she was sucked down into a deep and dreamless sleep from which she did not wake until the 'plane was approaching the English coast.

'You missed your supper,' said Mrs Hannay quietly. 'I decided not to wake you, you looked much too happy, wherever you were.'

Emily was reluctant to move from the awkward yet comfortable position in which she had been sleeping. The lights in the 'plane had been turned down and there was little sound other than the thrust of the jets and the occasional movement of the air hostess in response to a call.

'How much longer?' Emily asked.

'Twenty minutes or so,' Mrs Hannay replied.

Mrs Hannay was sitting with her seat upright reading a book, the title of which Emily could not see. She looked fresh and alert as though she had managed to have a good rest earlier in the day. Her right hand holding the book in front of her was quite steady. Emily watched her discreetly from beneath half closed eyelids. There was something about the way Mrs Hannay was sitting and holding up the book that suggested strength of will and quiet courage. Emily remembered that Mrs Hannay had escaped from Russia as a girl not much older than herself. What dull lives children in England had to lead! The spring term would start in three days unless there was a war or a revolution.

'Ladies and gentlemen, we are now starting our approach to Gatwick Airport. Please fasten your seat belts and return your seats to the upright position.'

The lights of England: those are the suburbs of London away to the right and those below are the small towns and villages of Kent. Small houses with few lights. Safe, cosy country where nothing happens. Except school. With the courage that distance allows, Emily told herself that she half wished they had been trapped in the Winter Palace. What a challenge it would have been to find a way out. Unlike Alyce, who would have been all for breaking the windows and calling for help, she would have searched for the secret passage that led to the river. It would not have been easy to find but with the small pocket torch that she had taken to Russia to read by under the bedclothes, she would have explored behind all the closed doors. The entrance would have been behind a mirror or a bookcase. The cobwebs in the passage would already have been broken by whoever came and went to steal the Leonardo and at the river end there would have been a dangerous jump down on to the ice. If the ice had broken, that might have been the end until the ice melted in the spring and they found your body floating up to the surface like something they thought they had forgotten long ago.

'Fasten your seat belt, Emily,' said Alyce, looking round from the seats in front.

Gatwick Airport at half past midnight on a January morning was almost deserted. The travellers from Leningrad waited for their luggage in silence or, if they spoke, spoke in whispers as if they were awaiting the arrival of a royal personage. The British Customs was a perfunctory affair, not a case opened, hardly a question asked. You could have walked in with the Dubinsky Madonna under your arm for all they cared. Emily experienced a keen sense of disappointment. It had been the last chance for something dramatic to happen.

And there was Daddy. He was standing alone, looking rather dazed as though the last 'plane to civilisation had just left without him.

'Hallo Daddy.'

Emily was the last to greet him. He said: 'I'm surprised you weren't arrested, Emily.'

'Why?' she asked sharply. The old joke had a cutting edge.

'Oh, just you, Emily, just you,' he replied.

Mrs Hannay was introduced and offered a lift to London. But she was being met by her son and daughter-in-law. They said goodbye to her collectively. Emily wanted to say something different, to convey a message that would tell Mrs Hannay she knew everything and that she didn't think it wrong or criminal; on the contrary, she wished her luck. But the opportunity passed too quickly and a few minutes later her father was turning the car out of the airport approach on to the London road. It was raining.

Big Ben struck two as they crossed Westminster Bridge. In the glare and shadow of the city's lights, the river was flowing easily on the flood tide. The car drove into Dean's Yard and drew up in front of a Regency house in the corner by the Great College Street gate. Wearily, the family carried their cases upstairs, happy to be home again yet somewhat stunned by the changes of the journey.

'Don't unpack, dears,' their mother told them, 'go straight to bed.'

Emily opened her bedroom door and turned down the switch. In the harsh light, familiar objects looked strange. She lifted her case on to the bed and unlocked it. Somewhere within was her nightdress. She opened the lid. On the top of the jumble of clothes lay a flat, rectangular package in white paper about the size of a foolscap exercise book.

Nineteen

❧

Such a conflict of emotions was released by the sight of that package that Emily did not hear her mother coming along the corridor and opening the bedroom door.

'You should be in bed now darling, you must be dead tired.'

Instinctively, Emily turned to place herself between her mother and the contents of the case.

'I was just looking for my night-dress.'

'Two minutes,' said her mother, advancing to give Emily a kiss on the forehead 'and sleep on in the morning.'

'Goodnight Mummy, thank you for a lovely holiday.'

Her mother closed the door. Still holding the lid of the case open, Emily looked down again, half expecting that the white package would have gone, a trick of the tired mind; no more. But there was no escape from reality that way. She touched the white paper and felt the firm, flat shape within. Then she tried to untie the simple bow in the string but her shaking fingers pulled the wrong ends. Impatiently, she started tearing the paper, leaving the string in position. The paper came away easily enough, revealing first the young girl's face and then the large, unattractive head of the Baby Jesus. Emily grasped the picture in both hands and held it up to the light. It was the Dubinsky Madonna.

And yet it was not. The illusion lasted no more than a fraction of a second. The print had firm backing but was neither framed nor glazed. The accuracy of the colours produced a remarkable likeness to the original. Emily

turned it over to look at the back. There was a small label and a white envelope caught between the string and the picture. The envelope was addressed to her.

She placed the print on the bedcover as carefully as if it had been the Leonardo itself and then sat down beside it to open the envelope. The letter inside was in neat, small handwriting. It read:

My dear Emily,
I am writing this in the hotel before we leave for the airport. I have been shopping this afternoon. I did not know what to give you both for helping me to enjoy at least one evening to myself in the city where I was born. I wonder if you knew how much it meant to me to be able to

talk to my own people without Mr Oblamov in attendance. Poor Mr Oblamov! I'm afraid he will probably make a great fuss at the airport if only to save face with his superiors. But it will have been worth it, thanks to you. I really don't know what they are afraid of. I believe they tried to trick me into some indiscretion by sending me a note at the ballet. Wasn't that childish? And just for one moment I thought they suspected me of wanting to steal a painting — this painting — from the Winter Palace. It was rather flattering! The painting used to belong to our family. It is by Leonardo da Vinci. Do you remember it? It was in one of those galleries overlooking the river. You can imagine my surprise when I went there this morning to have a last look and found the painting had gone. It was silly of me, of course, but I really did imagine that after the circus Mr Oblamov had given instructions for the painting to be hidden until I was safely out of the country. How we all like to exaggerate our own importance! The explanation was much simpler. I asked one of the attendants. The Leonardo is on its way to Moscow for a special exhibition at the Tret'iakov Gallery.

Never mind — I found this copy in the House of Books. The colours are quite remarkably good don't you think? Hang it on your wall to remind you of your visit to Russia. I hope you will come here again one day. I don't suppose I shall be granted another visa, though I should dearly love to return, Mr Oblamov or no Mr Oblamov. Cherish your country, my dear, you do not know how much it means to you until you have lost it forever.

With my love to you both,

The letter was signed, 'Princess Natalya Nikolayevna Dubinsky.'

When she had turned out the light, Emily drew back the curtains and got into bed. She had placed the Madonna and Mrs Hannay's letter on the bedside table so that she could look at them again first thing in the morning.

For a few minutes she lay awake looking out of the window where, above the roofs, she could see the floodlit outline of Westminster Abbey. But when she closed her eyes she was looking at the ice on the River Neva and at the north face of the Winter Palace. The setting sun had already dropped out of sight, but above the line of dark statues and urns on the Palace roof the sky was as clear and blue as on a summer's day.

NOTE

In the State Hermitage Museum in Leningrad, which is housed in the former Winter Palace, there is a painting of Mary and the Baby Jesus by Leonardo da Vinci which is known as the Benois Madonna. It came to Russia in the Nineteenth Century with a group of Italian actors and was bought by the Benois family. The picture was studied by European experts and declared to be an authentic Leonardo. Tsar Nicholas II agreed to buy it for the Hermitage Museum, but when the Revolution broke out in 1917 only one instalment had been paid to the Benois family. The painting became the property of the new Communist State.

I have not used the name Benois because I do not know whether members of the family still live in Leningrad or elsewhere and, as this is just a story, I have no wish to take anybody's name in vain.